THIRST

UpSet Press

PO Box 200340
Brooklyn, NY 11220

www.upsetpress.org

Established in 2000, UpSet Press is an independent, not-for-profit (501c3 tax-exempt) press
based in Brooklyn. The original impetus of the press was to upset the status quo
through art and literature. The Press has expanded its mission to promote new work by new authors;
the first works, or complete works, of established authors—placing a special emphasis on
restoring to print new editions of exceptional texts; and first time translations of works into English.
Overall, UpSet Press endeavors to advance artists' innovative visions and works that
engender new directions in art and literature.

Library of Congress Control Number **2019947992**
ISBN 978-1-937357-84-9
Printed in the United States of America

BOOK DESIGN AND CHAPTER ARTWORKS : JESSICA D'ELENA-TWEED

THE

RICH

THIRST

ARE

VAMPIRES

ᵛ ᵛ ᵛ

NICHOLAS POWERS

THANK YOU, OCCUPY WALL STREET,
FOR SPARKING THE IDEA FOR THIS NOVEL.

PUERTO RICO

Down in the Southlands

One

BLOOD STAINED THEIR SHOES.

Another goat was found shredded by claws. The villagers circled it and pointed at the forest. Whatever killed their livestock came at night. Three identical men called the Roman brothers, poked at the dirt with their guns. Silently the people looked at them. And judged. Were they going to do anything?

A loud woman, dragged her daughter to the crowd. She elbowed her way to the front. It was Mariposa. Nervously, the Romans chewed sugar cane and spat in the grass.

"Are we going to wait until this thing kills one of our children?" She pointed at the goat. "Or kill, it?"

They tugged their straw hats and thought of her nice house. It looked like a giant sea-shell on the hill and eclipsed their tiny, zinc-roofed homes. When her old husband died, she got his land and walked, head up and looked men straight in the eyes. Flaunting his money, she drilled demands into their ears, "Do this, do that."

"We will trap it," the eldest Roman said. "And wait."

"Besides this is for us to decide." The middle Roman poked the goat with his gun. "Go protect your girl."

They left and the villagers broke into small, whispering talk. Mariposa lifted up her daughter Elutaria and went home. Bobbing in her mother's arms, she saw villagers leaving red footprints as they walked away.

∨ ∨ ∨

"We are the only real men in town," the eldest Roman said. The brothers laughed and hammered a wood cage to the ground. A squealing pig was led into the trap by the town priest, Father Azzure. They asked him for a blessing. They liked him. Unlike the last priest, he did not scream about Hell on Sunday but sang with his eyes closed. He would lift his arms as if lost in a trance, and townsfolk giggled in their sleeves. The youngest Roman said he squeezed God's ass. The parishioners stared at him to shut up. Now the Romans were going to trap the predator that came from the forest.

"You are the Christ pig." The middle Roman poked the pig. "You will die for our sins."

Azzure smelled alcohol on them. He began to pray, and the drunk-est brother snatched his rosary. He stomped off, as the Romans drank more beer. Evening dropped like a curtain on the village. They waited

in an empty chicken shed as the pig slept. Bored and cold, they drank to keep warm, and laugh at the slowness of night. They woke up, heads throbbing with daylight as the pig squealed in the trap, untouched.

They wiped dust off their clothes. Nothing. They looked at the sleeping town in the pink morning light. How would the people react when the learned the trap did not work? Down the road, a woman ran towards them. The wife of the youngest Roman thrust her hands in the air.

"Our son, our son, our son!" she shouted.

He sprinted. His brothers followed. He kicked the front door open, zigzagged into the child's bedroom, and saw torn sheets. Raising fists to his temples, he screamed and fell to the floor. They tried to hold him, but he dashed outside and found claw marks that curved back into the forest. His child's shoe lay on the dirt.

He got a machete from the shed. His wife and brothers wrapped their arms around him, but he tore free, stampeded to the trees and cut. With each hack, he shouted his son's name. Scared birds flew to the sky. Neighbors watched this man, swing by swing, digging a tunnel into dark foliage, calling for his child.

Elutaria held the bullets as her mother checked the shotgun. They left their house and joined the Roman brothers at the forest's edge. They passed the sugarcane to her. The townspeople came from their homes with rifles, machetes, and bright torches. The deathly quiet was punctuated by the metallic clink of bullets entering chambers.

Father Azzure muttered a prayer. In the torchlight, the men looked like they wore stone masks under which furtive eyes moved. Two by two, they marched into the forest becoming silhouettes under blazing yellow torches. Further in, the torch light flickered between the long branches.

When they didn't come back that night the wives and aunts, sisters, and mothers yelled for their men at the edge of the forest. Some sat on the ground like large breathing stones. In the morning, the woman glistened with dew and stray spider webs, not moving until Azzure came and lifted them gently to church.

They vowed to wait with the children, but desperation wrung their spirits like rags. One by one a mother or aunt or sister, gingerly stepped into the forest. They pulled hair from sweaty foreheads and stared into the thick knot of trees. Visions of their men being torn apart by the predator inside, throbbed like a waking nightmare. They stared into the forest, whose trees were rustled by the breeze, as if made of music.

At the end of the week, Father Azzure and a few children were left. They huddled in the church. He nailed crosses to the doors and sprinkled holy water on the ground. If Father Azzure wanted Elutaria to get food from the basement, she repeated a prayer as she descended into the dark. Her heart was like a horse kicking in her chest.

At night, he lit candles and counted the shrinking pile of food. They stood on pews and peeked through stain-glass windows at the forest. It looked like dark seaweed, the trees swayed as if underwater.

When the food ran out, Azzure left to scavenge empty homes. He told them to lock the door and only open up, if it was him. He kissed their foreheads and went out with a large sack slung over his shoulders. He never returned.

Each child was driven by hunger to leave. One day Elutaria woke up and knew she was alone. The sounds trampled by people's voices rose like strange music. Wind whistled between cracks of doors. Holy cloth on the pulpit flapped like the slaps they gave to mules. The church was a creaking thing, almost alive in how it seemed to bend in the wind.

Elutaria kneeled at the front door and hammered wooden boards over it. She peeked through cracks into the blinding daylight, at the trees that swayed like a woman's hair.

She pressed her eyeball to the doorframe to examine the forest for any sign of her mother. She hit the boards with her hands. She yelled until her voice broke. Pressing her lips against a wall, she made a silent plea to God.

Days later, Elutaria knew she was dying. Her belly was a black hole. She could barely lift her arms. Her lips were dry sand. If she didn't leave the church, she would die. She tugged at the wood that crisscrossed the door, until one plank fell. The loud crash on the floor hurt. She bent another plank back but was too weak to get it down and collapsed. She got up. She pulled. Late into the night, the last one came down. Elutaria opened the church door. Night wind made the sweat on her arms tingle. Rising from the forest was laughter.

She took weak steps toward the cackling. The dark forest sounded like a party. The full moon was a bright, stone eye.

I can hear you.

She smiled at the thought of seeing her family. Elutaria stumbled to the trees arms up, hands out, as if she was going to hug someone. On the earth, shadows glided in fast circles. She looked up. Dark shapes swam in the sky like sharks. They wrestled over something that ripped and fell to the ground. It was the upper torso of the youngest Roman. He looked at her in numb agony. He touched his arm socket, it looked like dried bread. His hand fell off in a cascade of glittery sand.

A shadow from the sky swooped down and squatted near him. It was Father Azzure. He hissed through a mouth of needle teeth, and his eyes were large like an insect's. He chomped the Roman brother and lifted him by the neck to the sky, where he was tossed between shark-like shadows, attacking in a feeding frenzy.

Elutaria froze. She took a step back and fell. On the ground, she blankly looked at her friends being torn apart in the sky. Her mouth twisted into a crazy grin. A severed head thumped onto the earth, bounced, and rolled nearby. Its eyes moved in the sockets as if confused. Elutaria laughed and laughed. She ripped out her hair and placed tufts of it into its open mouth.

"Eat. Eat," she giggled.

Farmers from the next village found her. She was nearly skeletal. In her fists were torn out patches of hair. They gave her water and food, but no matter what they did, she wouldn't stop laughing.

NEW YORK

Sine Sensu

this is not how i am
when i was a child, i had a fever
my hands felt just like two balloons

now i've got that

& komforte

in
not sight

understand

now i've got that

feeling once again

i have become komforte

i can't explain
you would not understand

this is not how i am
when i was a child, i had a fever
my hands felt just like two balloons

THE SEVEN PRINCIPAL LINES.

1. LINE OF SELF HATE.   2. LINE OF DUALITY.   3. LINE OF SECOND SIGHT.
4. LINE OF CRUELTY.   5. LINE OF SUFFERING.   6. LINE OF WANDERING.
7. LINE OF DELUSION.

Two

"COME ON FIND YOUR PILLS."

Maz aimed the flashlight into her bag. She shook it but did not hear the bottle. Panic corkscrewed her chest. How long before the last dose wore off? will the voices return?

"My locker," she giggled. "You stupid cunt, the pills are in your locker. Okay. Okay. You know where they are. Okay." Maz unzipped the tent and stepped on the empty roof. Beer bottles shined in moonlight. Thank God the building was abandoned. Less chance of rape. She'd squatted in it for weeks, and it almost felt like home.

Did anyone know where she was? No. And no one cared. I mean who wants a crazy, schizophrenic daughter? especially, one who hears voices? And she always heard voices. When her first period spotted her panties, whispers rose like steam on a cold day, and repeated the word, "thirst." Her first day as a woman was spent banging her head on a wall.

Thirst. Thirst. Thirst.

When she heard them as a child, Maz filled the bath, and dunked herself. Face wobbly under the water, she breathed through a plastic straw until her mom found her. Of course she asked what the hell was going on. Maz never had a good answer.

Thirst. Thirst. Thirst.

During the full moon the voices pecked at her skull like birds. Maz dreaded those bright nights when her brain shook and jumped. Once she stumbled out of the apartment and asked a police officer for help. The voices clawed reality into shreds. Her mind snapped.

Maz went to the hospital. She woke up with a needle in her arm and a liquid-filled bag on a medical stand next to her. The psychotropic drugs floated like a chunk of ice behind her eyes. She loved the numbness. Loved it.

After she was released, no one forced her to take medicine. Maz downed the pills like candy. It gave her points with the other zonked out kids at school. Maz bought an Incredible Hulk Pez dispenser, packed it with the blue pills, slammed it on the lunch table, and growled like Hulk in the *Avengers* movie.

Sometimes, she sold pills to freshman. They were dumb junkies in training. The seniors wanted them for "blackout" parties, where people filled bowls with many colored pills, and just randomly swallowed them with vodka. They said her pills were the best, made their heads float like balloons.

Her side business got her good pocket-money until a school guard came to class and called her. Maz felt the stares of everyone in the room draped over her like a heavy fishing net. In the principal's office, her mother sat, legs crossed, arms crossed, eyes hot with rage. "I'm fucked," Maz thought. The principal unzipped another student's bag and took out her blue pills. *Was she selling her medicine? Did she think this was a joke?*

Maz lied. She lied so well, she was proud of herself. She said the pills had been missing from her bag but she didn't want to get be seen as a "snitch". They half-believed her until she faked tears and wailed that she couldn't live without her meds. Why would anyone take them? The principal patted her shoulder and said she was safe now. Afterwards in the hall, her mom leaned in so close that her breath fogged Maz's glasses.

"Puta! Think your fucking Oscar performance fooled me?" She twisted Maz's collar tight, let go and stomped off.

When Maz came home, she opened the apartment door slowly. On her bed was a packed suitcase. A note taped to it said, "Go". She stood blinking as if being pulled apart with giant tweezers. Home? Gone. Mother? Gone. Life? Gone.

She lugged her suitcase to the street. It bumped each stair like a lead ball. Her neighbors looked away. Maz stood on the sidewalk, make-up like dark rain on her face, and trembled with rage. Her friend Sheena, texted her to come over.

The subway ride to East New York was a blur. Eyes closed, she remembered Dolores spinning her finger at her temple cuckoo-style and staring at Maz. Once she twisted the radio knob to different channels and said it was Maz. Another time, she stared at Maz for a long, hateful time and said she should have aborted her. Now she was finally a thrown-away girl like out of some Charles Dickens' novel. A strange relief filled her.

Maz found Sheena's building and hauled her suitcase past sleepy-eyed boys smoking a blunt on the stoop. The halls were like peeled skin, and "Jesus Loves You" signs hung on doors. Maz knocked on '3A'. Sheena opened the door and looked at her friend. They hugged.

At dinner, Maz sat with Sheena, Sheena's mom, and steptfather. Of course she could stay. And not to worry. Maz tried to thank them but choked on tears as they rubbed her shoulders.

After dinner, Maz slept on the couch. At night, car lights flashed across the room and leaning on the wall was the stepfather. He rubbed his crotch while staring at Maz, then left. She packed her suitcase, got on a bus, and hauled it through a neighborhood of empty buildings. Maz cracked open a window, its broken glass like jagged teeth on the floor. Squirming through it, she threw her luggage inside.

Thirst. Thirst. Thirst.

Maz pressed hands on her temples. Please stop, just stop, I can't right now, I just fucking can't. Maz punched her head.

Thirst. Thirst. Thirst. Thirst.

˅ ˅ ˅

Yo! Maz is here.

Damien's text rolled down the cellphone screens of Consuela, Freddie Fly, Co-Co, and Maurice. They were the hormone-driven, terrorist seniors that ran Brooklyn's Bushwick High. When they walked, freshman and sophomores flattened on walls to let them pass. It was their last month at school and they called it "Survival of the Illest", a riff on Social Darwinism that they half-learned in History class.

Damien was the chiseled baller who held freshman down and smashed his senior ring into their foreheads. They bore the imprint like an Ash Wednesday mark. Freddie Fly, spray-painted nerds, marking an 'X' on clothing he said was "gay as shit". They begged him to

stop, but he caught them in a MMA-style chokehold. And then out would come the spray paint! Co-Co and Consuela taped airplane vomit bags on the lockers of fat girls with a letter that read, "Go Bulimic!" And Maurice would just randomly and without reason, punch a freshman in the eye or jaw because he could.

Few slid under their radar. They terrorized the whole school. Yet, in some sad Stockholm Syndrome way, they were loved by the students they bullied. Maz saw freshman, sophomores, even juniors, dress and talk like their torturers. Maz kept her distance but eyed Co-Co and Consuela with contempt. They picked up on it. Narcissistic teen-psychopaths, can sense the smallest ripple of judgement. So they planned a "prank".

Maz was a drug-popper and a small-time peddler but then again, who wasn't? Everyone had a "condition" that needed medicine. It could be ADD or "social anxiety" or whatever new label the industry slapped on a confused kid to pimp them for money. Consuela heard that Maz was supposed to be a full-blown schizo, the crown jewel of disorders. They began to plot a Darwin Award because taking out the mentally ill was a gift to humanity.

"We don't want her breeding crazies." Co-Co coiled a strand of hair on her finger, and studied Maz at lunch. The rest nodded.

Steal her pills and watch her pop. Damien hired a student to get them. They waited. Maz dug in her locker for pills. He texted a photo to the crew. Consuela laughed hard and replied

Every day she reeks. Let dogs lick you. Do something. You burn my nose hairs bitch.

Laugh emoji flashed on their screens.

I heard from my boyz in her last school that she puts on a fucking show nigga, her head will spin like the Exorcist.

Consuela said whoever sees her pop gets free drinks at her bar.

Damien sent photos of Maz deep in her locker. Notebooks fell as she rifled around. In the next photo she leaned against the locker and covered her face. The last one showed her running away, half in the frame, half out.

In the next class their phones buzzed. Freddie Fly sent a photo of Maz in the backrow wearing a pair of astronaut-sized earphones. Next they saw Maz in the hallway, head down with hands pressed to her ears. Five minutes later, Consuela sent a message.

She's popping!

They saw a photo of Maz's screaming. Maz hurling her desk at the teacher. Maz tackled by security, one of her hands reaching above their hunched backs. Maz being wrapped in a straightjacket like a mummy and lifted to a gurney. Maz yelling as she was wheeled through the hall, and the whole school crammed at doorways, staring at her. Consuela texted.

You all are buying me drinks!

Later that night, Consuela laughed as a man fanned dollar bills at her ass. He slapped her oiled cheeks as she scooped up the cash and scissor-walked offstage. Older strippers studied her hourglass body, dark wavy hair, and the cash dangling from her G-string. Her youth made their C-section scars and loose breasts uglier. She took all the men. She took all the money. They hated her.

Consuela sarcastically blew them a kiss. They scrunched their faces. One shot her a middle finger. More men walked into the Playpen Strip Club. Grizzled Mexican and Pakistani immigrants with jittery eyes, desperate to feel they had something a woman wanted. They sat and ordered drinks as the girls played with their shirt buttons. Smiling like babies, the men opened their wallets.

Consuela stirred the straw in her pink cocktail and bored, scrolled through her cellphone. "Fuck you, right?"

She whipped around. A man held palms up and smiled mischievously.

"It's what the hags said to you." He slid into the seat next to her.

"What can you expect?"

She scanned him. Mid-thirties. Clean. Urban but not thug. Coffee-tone skin. Some kind of Black Latino? Speaks like money. Cute.

"Yes," she smiled like a lightbulb. "Haters will hate." She touched his knee. "What's your name baby?"

"Charlemagne." He stroked her arm. "Maybe a private dance?"

The manager absentmindedly waved as he walked by, went to the office, and put a slice of pizza near the video monitor. On it Consuela sat alone. But acted as if she talked with someone. She rose and parted the curtains of the private dance room. The screen blacked out.

"Is this good?" she asked.

Charlemagne peeled off a hundred dollar bill from a fat roll of cash. She straddled him and winced at the icy cold of his skin. Money was money. She ground her hips on him. He gripped her waist like a steel vice and kissed her hard.

She tried to squirm free, but he stopped her. A wave of energy rolled through her, and she fell to the floor. It was hard to breathe. Did he punch her in the gut? She screamed. No sound came out. She reached for her throat, it collapsed in her hand as dust.

Oh my God! Oh my God! Oh my God!

She reached for the seat, and each finger cracked apart. The arm collapsed. The empty socket looked like dry, crumbled bread.

Charlemagne stood. She lifted her hand to stop him. Fingers blew apart like sand. Quietly he stomped her feet, stomped her legs into dust, hips into dust, chest and shoulders into dust. His foot was aimed above her face. And then it fell.

Afterwards, he picked up Consuela's G-string and put it in his pocket. Leaving the club, he slipped past women plying the drunk men. One stripper passed him as she went upstairs and entered the manager's door. He tapped the blacked-out surveillance screen. It turned on, showing Consuela's drink near the stage.

∨ ∨ ∨

Wake up...

Blinking, Maz looked at I.V. tubes taped to her arms. Her body was wrapped in a hospital bedsheet. Oh God, am I here again?

Look at me...

Consuela sat on the bed and rubbed the hole in her throat. Grains of dust fell on the bed. Maz froze. Her breath was a big rock in her lungs. Consuela made a stay-quiet gesture.

Can you hear me?

"Your throat..." she began, "what happened to your..."

They are watching us. They have since the beginning of time.

"Who are you talking about?" Maz yelled. "What the fuck is going on Consuela? Why are you here? Why is there a fucking hole in your throat?"

Consuela put a finger to Maz's mouth, stood her up, and led her into the hallway. One end was pitch black. Maz pulled the I.V. stand and babbled questions. They walked into the shadows, until the hospital was a faint light far behind them. Cold wind blew.

I don't have a lot of time left. They are draining me. But you know who "they" are. You have been hearing them your whole life.

She let go of Maz.

They don't know you can hear them. Listen. Learn. Kill them before the Awakening. They are thirsty.

Maz woke up in the hospital bed.

At Bushwick High School, no one waved at Maz. Students hung their heads like sad flowers. What was going on? Wasn't anyone going to laugh at her? The schizo girl has returned people! Come on! Let's make her life a living hell! But they passed her as if she was invisible. A pimpled kid who bought her blue pills, gave a cheerleader famous for having multiple abortions, a large flowery card to sign. Did someone die?

Maz wasn't ready for this scene. On Friday, she had been released from the hospital. The car ride home was silent. Dolores sat grim behind the wheel. When they reached their building, Maz lugged her suitcase up to her room and sat on her bed. Am I such a failure that I can't even run away right?

Laying on her back, Maz imagined her "friends" snickering behind her back. She gulped down a fistful of pills. No more voices. No more giving a shit what those losers at that breeding ground for Bell Curve babies think. And Monday came.

"You're a tough bitch." Maz stared at her reflection. "You're a tough bitch."

She studied her coffee-brown face, dark, straight hair, and little pig nose…Cute almond-shaped eyes. Each feature on its own was cute. But on her face, they looked plain. Fuckable is how guys appraised her. Fuckable.

"Well Ms. Fuckable is going back to get her shitty diploma," she said.

Maz took the bus to school, held her breath, and pushed open the doors. And no one said "Hi". No one even noticed her. A crowd stood near a locker. The pimply kid and cheerleader put a large card on the floor.

Maz's heart closed like a fist. On the floor, electric candles throbbed near Consuela's face.

"She just disappeared. Like that." A pimply girl snapped her fingers. "Her mother called every living creature on this planet. Police. Politicians. Nothing. She's gone yo." She shook her head. "No one's safe in this city. This is like the fifth person this week. Right?"

"The police have no fucking clue." A boy next to her nodded.

Maz stepped away and palmed her forehead. Did I not hallucinate Consuela in the hospital? The memory came into focus. Yes, she had seen Consuela next to her bed, touching a hole in her throat.

They have been watching us since the beginning.

Blinking at the memory, Maz studied the electric candle altar. How could I know? How did she? But there's no way.

The bell rung. The crowd broke apart. Maz hugged her books to her chest, and squinted at the photos. No. No. No. It was a hallucination that's all, I was tripping on my medicine. She halted, mid-step. Students rolled their eyes and walked around her. Wait. I wasn't even on the new medicine.

She took out her Hulk Pez dispenser and thumbed it open. Each one kept her safe from herself. If she went full schizo? Holy shit. Schizos have cut themselves. Or bashed a dad's head in with a hammer.

But Consuela? It was just a hallucination. Was it? She didn't know. She wouldn't know unless she stopped taking the pills.

They don't know you can hear them. Listen. Learn. Kill them before the Awakening.

Maz closed the Hulk Pez dispenser. She didn't see the tall, dark-eyed boy with a red bandana, staring at her from the doorway. When she left for class. He lingered, then followed her.

HEAVEN.
EARTH.
HELL.

HATE.
HAVEN.

IF I'M YOU, OR YOU ME

INTERPENETRATING GOD

ENLARGING INTIMACY.

YOU WHO ARE

ANIMUS

AND BLOOD

WHO MAKE ME INTO DUST

BLOWN INTO GRASS

INVISIBLE — IS IT YOU, OR I

I PASS AND CANNOT SEE?

Three

CHARLEMAGNE STEPPED ON THE BUILDING LEDGE.

In the streets below, cars looked like ants in a maze. Icy wind lashed buildings. Rain whipped him.

Thirst. Thirst. Thirst.

The dry ache in his mouth spread to his throat. The bright moonlight caressed his body, and a low electrical hum traveled along his nerves. He jumped and hung suspended in air. First he tore off coat, pants, and shirt. They fell like rags into the street.

The moonlight erased him. Only his shadow moved on the side of the building. He flew on wind and lingered above a balcony. Teens drank beer and joked about sex. Young fear rose from their bodies and tasted like cotton candy to Charlemagne. It was delicious. He wanted to drain it from them.

A young woman stood alone and saw his shadow on the wall. She touched it and turned side to side. No one could throw a shadow that high up. The drink shook in her hand.

Charlemagne was startled. No one noticed their shadows on the walls, floors and ceilings. Few were that observant. She traced it again, and when he moved, his shadow moved and she dropped her drink.

He flew around the building, and scraped the brick with fingertips. The city was a blurry light under rain clouds. Towers poked out, dark stone against dark night, checkered by lit up rooms, and inside people moved like miniature dolls. One brightly lit apartment had an old man inside, cooking dinner. Charlemagne landed inside the apartment.

Thirst. Thirst. Thirst.

Jose liked the rice burned. He stirred the pot, waiting for it to cook, and hummed a salsa tune. A door slammed. His heart jumped, and he ran to look. The balcony was empty. Nothing broken. Everything was quiet.

He shrugged and went back to the kitchen. The stove was turned off. The spoon he used to stir was licked clean and on the counter.

"What the hell!" Jose backed up.

The lights went off. He screamed. After a few seconds, he picked up a lighter on the table. In a quick thumb stroke. It flicked on.

A shadow loomed on the wall. It belonged to something tall and thin. The lighter singed his fingertips. Jose shook it cool and flicked it

on. A man stood nose to nose with him. The lighter snuffed out. The balcony doors opened. Dust blew out of the apartment.

"Sorry about the drink." Maz left to get a towel.

The guys shot scornful glances at her. Two made the crazy sign, spinning their finger around their temples, mouthing "Cuckoo, Cuckoo." Another two—Raffie, a thick-armed man, shook his head at Jesus, a tall, quiet teen who nervously tugged his bandana.

"Bro, why'd you bring her?" Raffie planted his big hands on his chest.

"You already bought the pills from her. Why bring the crazy bitch? She's a fucking spaz! I don't want her going schizo in my space."

Jesus stared into his beer.

"What if she goes full retard?" Raffie drilled him. "Police come, see all our shit. The fuck you thinking?" They locked eyes. A quiet challenge pulsed. The group held their beers, waiting to see if a fight was going to pop.

"I'll take her home," Jesus mumbled.

"Do that." Raffie turned his back.

Jesus found Maz in the bedroom, working arms into coat sleeves. He watched her hold a Hulk Pez dispenser, thumbed it open as if to take a pill. She saw him and jumped.

"Jesus." she blinked, palmed her chest.

"That's me," he smirked.

Maz shook her head as if to say 'You-Are-An-Idiot'. Shouldering her purse, she squeezed past him to the hall. He followed.

"What's up," she grimaced "you want something? I'm not going to towel it up. I know they didn't even want me at their party."

"I'll just walk you to the train," he leaned on the wall.

"No!" her lips tightened.

He put his coat on. Checked his cellphone. Pushed the elevator button.

"I said no," she snapped.

He stared at her in bewilderment. "You heard about the kidnappings...right?"

Maz shot him a dirty stare. Jesus fished a beer from his pocket. Fumbled for his opener. She bit her lip, shook her head.

"You know that's a really fucked up thing to say. Really. Fucked. Up." Maz pointedly gave him the shoulder.

He pushed the elevator button again.

"Please stop that." She stared at him, dramatically blinking.

"Nerves," he mumbled.

"Nerves?" She palmed her forehead like a theater actress.

"My luck, we'll both be kidnapped." He fidgeted his red bandana. "Be nice to have candles in front of my locker."

The elevator came and they went in. Maz waited. He stared at the ceiling. She played with her coat buttons and waved at the security camera.

"Do you think anyone would notice if we disappeared?" she asked in an airy voice.

Jesus raised his eyebrows, shrugged, and took a swig. He wiped his mouth with his sleeve, burped.

"Are you an alcoholic?" she asked.

"No," he smiled. "But I am trying. Who knows, if I put in the effort, I may be one of the greats." He took another swig. "Like Charles Bukowski."

Maz held out her hand. Jesus passed her the beer, and watched her drain it dry in one long gulp.

"Try harder." She threw it.

Jesus choked on laughter. Maz patted him on the back. They stepped out of the elevator, left the building but a blast of icy wind

forced them to huddle in a doorway. She shivered. He took off his hoodie. She half-fought him as he pulled it down over her. Her shaking stopped. White breath puffed like geysers from their mouths.

"Oh my god, our breath is so alcoholic." She poked the plume of his exhale. "We could light it on fire."

He took his lighter, and she reached for it.

"C'mon," he teased.

"Fucker." She elbowed him playfully. "Hold it still."

Thirst. Thirst. Thirst.

Charlamagne glittered with the old man's dust. He circled the sky above New York like a shark sniffing for blood. Below him, two teens played with a lighter in the doorway. Up, up, up he went into the night.

Shadows lit by the moon made dark shapes inside clouds. The Coven swam in the sky and followed the scent of fear to drain. A jolt in their brains startled them and they spiraled down to a ruined church outside the city. They landed on its roof and became visible. Crawling along the walls, they went deep into the basement. Cold eyes flashed in the dark.

Thirst. Thirst. Thirst.

Deep into the bowels of the church, they crawled over each other in frantic need. A bottomless ache swelled in their mouths.

Thirst, thirst, thirst.

At the end, a large underground hall was filled with their soft grunts. They all heard the call from The First One, it was the oldest and most powerful of them. Its voice was a warm waterfall. Peace. Jostling in the deep, they stepped on glittery sand dunes. Each figure kneeled, and poured sparkly grains or coughed some out or wiped it from their skin. One had an urn and bent on her knees to add it. Others scooped

handfuls to rub on their faces. Others scraped it on limbs as if to wash off sin.

Everyone came with need. Charlemagne gave the crystalized energy he drained from the old man. When the last grain fell, a hypnotic pulse sparked in his brain. It was like a giant strobe-light that blasted away thought. It blinded him to anything but the terrible, needed beauty of The First One.

Close-eyed, he walked to the pulsing light. Inside a back chamber, a dried corpse-like thing lay on the cement. Its face was a wrinkled prune. Its eyeballs, rotten eggs. It lightly breathed, and inside the rib cage its lungs were small balloons. The First One was drawing energy from their offerings. It bound them across space and time. It kept their memories safe, even when during the times of thirst, the Coven forgot its own history. Weeping, Charlemagne fell on his knees in front of the figure.

The Light. The Light. The Light. It was sweet pain. The strobe quickened into a long continuous stream. He rejoiced and then it pushed him away. Hard, heavy waves knocked him back. He woke up on top of a dune and saw others were being called, and going in to see The First One.

As Charlemagne left the church, he bumped shoulders with those coming in. He squeezed his head. Memories of lifetimes rushed in. Yes. The stars. Yes. They began in the stars. They flew through space in a hive until this planet called them. Yes. They crashed here. Yes. They stole the bodies of these smelly animals. Flesh was heavy. Air was heavy. Sunlight was heavy. Thought was heavy. Existence was weight.

Fast images crashed in on him like floodwater. Eyes clenched: he had been a tribal chief, dressed in furs, who dragged a child into a cave, and drained it to dust. And a noblewoman in the royal garden chewing the neck of a chambermaid. And a Nazi at a concentration camp licking ash from the ovens. And a Vietnam War soldier biting a prisoner into

dust. He saw the centuries he spent on Earth, roaming from host body to host body, constantly thirsty, constantly on the hunt. He remembered who he was and who they were.

Charlemagne wanted The First One to call him again, but more dust was needed. He jumped on the ledge of the church's roof and saw the city like an electric anthill. The moon was a giant, stone eye. They could fly during the full moon. When it waned, they were too heavy, too blind and dumb. If he was to drain Essence, it had to be now. He jumped into the sky.

Thirst. Thirst. Thirst.

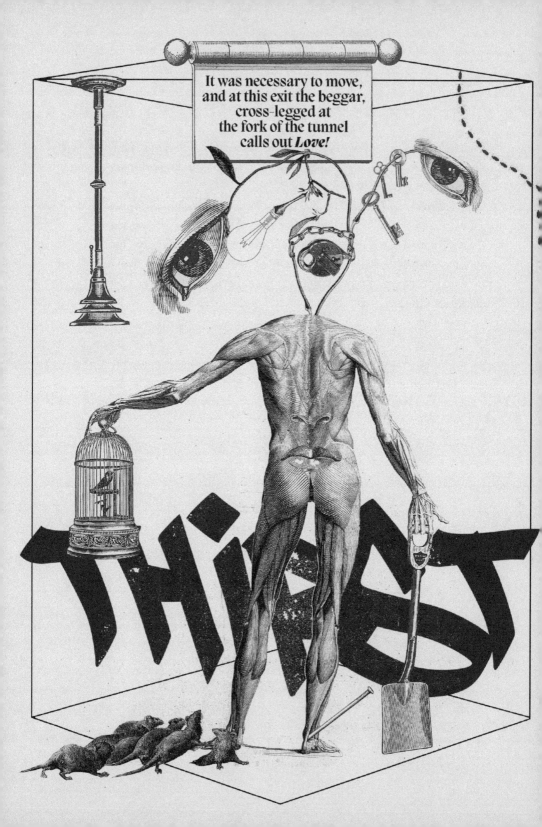

It was necessary to move,
and at this exit the beggar,
cross-legged at
the fork of the tunnel
calls out *Love!*

Four

"SO...WHAT HAPPENED BACK THERE?" Jesus asked.

Maz flipped the hood of her sweatshirt down to hide from the question. He peeked inside.

"Hello?"

"Sorry, no speak English," she said with an Asian accent.

"You better."

"Ooh!" she pulled the hoodie further down. "Sometimes I see things."

Maz waited for his lips to pucker or his eyebrows to snarl, some sign that he was afraid or disgusted. That's how people reacted when she unrolled the long scroll of Crazy. He made a keep-going motion with his hands.

"I'm schizophrenic. I hear things. I see things," she breathed as if deep diving. "I hear things. I take medicine. I love my medicine! I am alone a lot. I know that no one likes me. I don't know why you are treating me nice. I think it's because you want to fuck me. I am not interested in fucking. I don't want to hear you in my body. I am embarrassed to even say this. I give you permission to leave now."

He pushed the cowl of the hoodie back and she wheeled her arms blindly. Maz yanked it back down and saw him smiling.

"See," he said, "still here."

"You know I hear a voice right now." She clutched her head. "They are telling me to kick your ass into next week."

Giggling loosened their faces and they elbowed each other. The green bulb light of the subway station was ahead. Maz wondered if she could stall until they got there.

"Okay," Maz stopped and said. "While I was on the balcony at your dickhead friend's place. I saw a shadow..."

Jesus shrugged.

"It didn't belong to anyone," she blurted.

He titled his head, first to one side, then the other. They walked on. Faces sown up. Hers with shame. His with curiosity.

"You know that's what I tell myself," Maz sighed. "I say, Hey girl, it's the meds. No sweat. Don't trip. But I know when it's the pills."

Jesus squinted. "Why not chill on the pills?" He pointed at a homeless man with wild bushy hair. "Oh there's Picasso."

Picasso spat at them and went back to chalking an outline on the wall.

"He's always with these dumb cartoons," Jesus said.

Maz studied the ragged man. He plugged his ear with rags. She tapped him on the shoulder. Jesus tugged at her, but she shook him off. He wheeled around. Maz gestured to pull the dirty cloth.

"Take them out," she hollered.

Picasso ripped the rags from his ears.

"Now I hear them! Now I can, I can, I can hear all them! You loud. You loud and they know it." He wiped is face with his sleeve.

Jesus tugged at her. "C'mon, he's crazy."

"As if I'm not." Maz moved closer to Picasso. He shrank against the wall, where his chalk cartoons glowed like strange constellations. Maz watched him furiously draw a person floating above him. He struck the wall and chalked arrows in every direction. At the end of each he wrote, "Thirst." Maz felt her chest tighten.

"They make shadows," Picasso said. "No one sees. Shadows. They watch us. Thirsty, they thirst!"

Maz grabbed Jesus. "That's what I hear too." She jabbed the chalk figure. "I saw a shadow on the wall, but it didn't belong to anyone. It was above us. Ever since I was a girl, I heard voices say 'thirst'. My whole life."

⌄ ⌄ ⌄

Maz let the subway rock her like a baby. Tired. Tired. Tired. The dark sorcery of imagination began. Picasso's outlines ran, jumped, and flew like a cartoon scribbled by the insane.

She stared at the grimy tunnel as the 'A' train sped through it. So what's a girl to do? She took out her pills. Shook them. They rattled like dice. The memory of Jesus came back.

Why don't you chill on the pills?

When he asked, his voice lifted like he had stepped into a puddle. Maz felt guilty because he said something she'd been wanting to say for years. Live without the medicine. She held up the bottle and inside the pills were dark dots.

"Sis," a man said to her. "You selling?" He sat across from her. Maz sized him up. Olive face, curly high-top with eyes ringed by dark circles. Addict. New York's Finest. Well, what else can happen?

"You don't want any of this." She smiled crookedly. "It makes you see dead people."

He wiped his mouth and pulled out a $50 bill.

"All good," he cooed in a syrupy voice. "But if we doing this, it has to be now. Feel me?"

Maz didn't care about the money. No, she just needed to know what was real and what wasn't. Was there something going on? Some force beyond her schizophrenia? She tossed him the bottle and took the cash. He slid it inside his coat and left when the train whooshed into the station.

She crossed her arms and leaned over. So this is how it begins? A random drug deal on the train? Dear Oprah. Is this is how I live my best life? She giggled maniacally, crumpled the bill in her hand, and walked to the drunk. Plastic rum bottles rolled at his feet. She held the collar over her nose, held the pole, and leaned over.

"Thirst." Maz tucked the money into his shirt pocket.

⌄ ⌄ ⌄

The boy climbed the fence into the empty church to discover if the stories were true. Loud noises. Dry mouth as you got closer.

Azmi jumped down and quietly checked the entrance. Doors hung loose off hinges. One tilted like a broken tooth. He slipped inside.

Moonbeams slanted through the half-collapsed roof. Azim stepped on the bright circles on the floor like stones in a pond. He felt a touch on his cheek, spun and tore at a spider-web.

Azmi cursed, and his voice echoed in large rings that faded. He felt very small but wanted to have a story to tell his friends. Step by step he traveled down, until the blackness was so thick, he could almost taste how old the silence was.

A sizzling sound filled his ears. It came from the floor. He bent down and felt dust whizzing past his fingertips, minute grains that in the dark felt large and fast. It was as if he could see with touch.

A moaning rose and the sound traveled along Azmi's nerves. He bolted up the stairs, back out of the church, and out into the street. The moaning intensified, as if he had awakened whoever was inside.

∨ ∨ ∨

In the darkness, dust rippled in waves toward The First One. Its eyes inflated. Its ribcage filled with organs, and new skin rolled over, covering everything like a bandage.

The dust of slain people reanimated the First One, who coughed through a jaw that was re-stitching to its skull with the lace of new tendons. Every second was flame. Life was heavy. Every cell felt like an anvil. Under thin lids, its eyes moved like marbles.

Can you hear me?

The Coven shouted through the telepathy in joy. They called from across the nearby city and the far-flung continents.

Are you ready? Are you ready for the Awakening?

CAPITAL IS DEAD LABOUR, THAT, VAMPIRE-LIKE, ONLY
THE CAPITALIST THEN TAKES HIS STAND ON THE LAW
AND STRESS OF THE PROCESS OF PRODUCTION, RISES:
EXPANSION OF CAPITAL, IS ON MINE EXTRA
ACQUIRES IT. TO YOU, THEREFORE, BELONGS
WITH THE SAME NORMAL AMOUNT OF
SET IN MOTION, PUT INTO ACTION

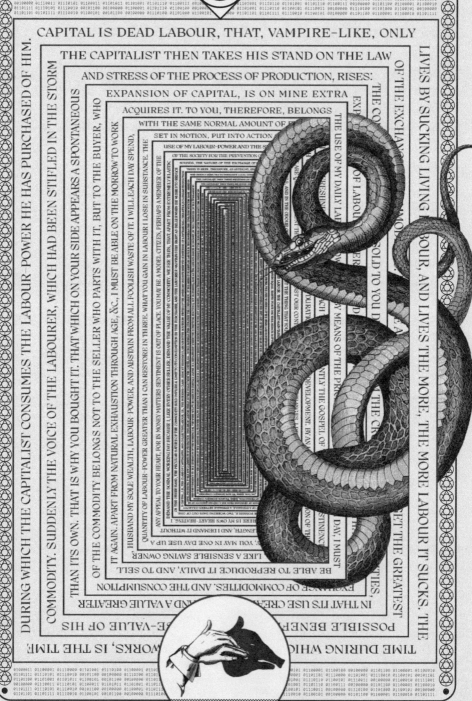

LIVES BY SUCKING LIVING LABOUR, AND LIVES THE MORE, THE MORE LABOUR IT SUCKS. THE

DURING WHICH THE CAPITALIST CONSUMES THE LABOUR-POWER HE HAS PURCHASED OF HIM.

COMMODITY. SUDDENLY THE VOICE OF THE LABOURER, WHICH HAD BEEN STIFLED IN THE STORM

THAN ITS OWN. THAT IS WHY YOU BOUGHT IT. THAT WHICH ON YOUR SIDE APPEARS A SPONTANEOUS

OF THE COMMODITY BELONGS NOT TO THE SELLER WHO PARTS WITH IT, BUT TO THE BUYER, WHO

IT AGAIN. APART FROM NATURAL EXHAUSTION THROUGH AGE, &c., I MUST BE ABLE ON THE MORROW TO WORK

HUSBAND MY SOLE WEALTH, LABOUR-POWER, AND ABSTAIN FROM ALL FOOLISH WASTE OF IT. I WILL EACH DAY SPEND,

QUANTITY OF LABOUR-POWER GREATER THAN I CAN RESTORE IN THREE. WHAT YOU GAIN IN LABOUR I LOSE IN SUBSTANCE. THE

ANY APPEAL TO YOUR HEART, FOR IN MONEY MATTERS SENTIMENT IS OUT OF PLACE. YOU MAY BE A MODEL CITIZEN, PERHAPS A MEMBER OF THE

LIKE A SENSIBLE SAVING OWNER

BE ABLE TO REPRODUCE IT DAILY, AND TO SELL

EXCHANGE OF COMMODITIES, AND THE CONSUMPTION

IN THAT ITS USE CREA... AND A VALUE GREATER

POSSIBLE BENEF... ...SE-VALUE OF HIS

TIME DURING WHIC... ...WORKS, IS THE TIME

Five

THE MOON WANED.

A plane blinked between clouds. A man held a fidgety boy by the collar and licked his lips.

"Charlemagne, can I go home?" he asked. The boy had the pinched look of Down Syndrome.

"Soon," he answered. "Miss your parents?"

The boy nodded. Fear hummed like electricity in his head. He didn't know the man. During the Penn Station rush hour, the crowds bumped him, and he lost his nurse. He cried her name and a large pair of hands yanked him into the 'A' train. The boy saw a smiling adult who asked if he was lost. Yes, yes he was. Okay, let's get you home. He said he was Charlemagne. They slept on the train. When the boy woke, they were in a station he'd never seen.

Charlemagne cooed gentle words. Everything was okay. He had a quick errand that brought them to this run-down brownstone. In the backyard he told the boy to close his eyes, and soon he'd be back home. The boy goofily smiled, palmed his face and counted.

"Keep counting..." He glanced around. The windows were boarded up. No lights on in any of the other empty homes. No cops. No pushers. No addicts. No one.

"Still counting?" Charlemagne wiped his mouth. The boy gave a thumbs up. He opened his mouth and rows of needle teeth sprouted. In one bite, he lifted the boy and tossed him like a small animal. The child screamed. At each swing, a limb sprayed into dust. His right arm, dust. His left arm, dust. His legs poured like sand out of his pants.

Empty clothes fell to the ground. Panting, Charlemagne rubbed glittery dust onto his face. He could feel again. He scooped up the boy's essence and laughed. His mouth sparkled like stars.

Thirst. Thirst. Thirst.

⌄ ⌄ ⌄

The moon waned to a sliver. The Coven stared at its scythe-like curve, as if the edge cut the telepathic web and plunged them into silence. In the time of thirst, none remembered who they were, brains went blank. Brutal hunger drove to hunt. They fed on the poor or outcast, until the full moon came again.

Thirst. Thirst. Thirst.

Dryness signaled the first stage. It struck randomly, maybe at a meeting, or in private. The moist throat parched into stone. Pain struck the nervous system like a match igniting. Cut off from each other, they staggered into the thirst.

In New York, during a morning police briefing, Officer Matos chewed his lip. The cop next to him pointed at his mouth. Matos touched it, and

a bright red drop of blood slipped down. He went to the bathroom and clawed his throat. Aridness seeped down his chest. He leaned on the toilet and gulped the water.

Thirst. Thirst. Thirst.

On Wall Street a stock broker coughed uncontrollably and jogged to her office. Closing the door, she fell on the floor, and gasped for air. Hot, baking pain shook her like a doll.

Thirst. Thirst. Thirst.

The CEO waved goodbye to the last accountant, closed the door, and clutched the curtains. Twisting them round himself, he muffled a scream. Every swallow was like swallowing glass.

Thirst. Thirst. Thirst.

ᕁ ᕁ ᕁ

Jesus scrolled through his cellphone. The news headlines said a Down Syndrome child was missing. Then it vibrated. He looked. Maz.

"What's up?"

"No more pills."

"..."

"Aren't you going to say something?" she barked. "Like 'Hey, you done good girl' or 'Thanks for taking my advice!'"

"..."

"Hello?"

"It's a lot Maz," he said it like a tide receding from shore.

"What you mean 'it's a lot Maz'?" she yelled. "You were all cheer-leading me to get off the meds."

"Oh I get it. If the psycho bitch goes crazy," she lashed out at him. "You don't want to know or you'll catch a case."

Jesus held the phone from his ear, and mouthed - Shut the fuck up.

"Goodbye Jesus!" She tried to hang up but pressed the wrong buttons.

Jesus heard Maz on the live call, and listened for a chance to apologize. She panted going up the stairs. A loud TV played a political ad where a deep-voiced man said, "We need to keep the Muslims out!"

"Mom, you're watching that again?" Maz raged. "What? You barely talk to me and you say that! Why do I come here? Because I live here! Because I'm your daughter! FUCK YOU! Really! Really! What do you do for me Mom?"

Jesus grimaced. This was not going good.

"How about this?" Maz slammed something loud. "Since you don't want to be my mom, I'll just call you The Bitch. I do it under my breath anyway. I call you The Bitch because we're not family. We're not, we haven't been in, I don't know, like forever. I used to care, I did but I don't now. I don't care if you never love me. No, I won't shut up! You shut up!"

Jesus squished the phone to his ear. Fear shot up as Maz cursed. Do I say something? Glass shattered. Silence. Another loud crash.

"Get away from me, or I swear I'll fucking stab you!" Maz screamed.

Oh shit. Jesus knew that crazy-wild, high sound. He saw bullied kids at school snap and go blind with rage. They were dangerous. They pulled a knife, or a gun. Maz was a split second away from doing something that could put her in prison.

"MAZ! PUT THE KNIFE DOWN!" he hollered.

"Jesus?" She grabbed her phone.

"Maz come to my place. Okay. Just leave," he said. "Just leave!"

Doors slammed. He heard Maz crying as she ran down the stairs. Cars honked. Wind. Muffled talk like a sluggish river.

"I'm so tired. I'm so tired. I'm so tired," she repeated in a sinking voice.

"Listen to me, I'm texting my address. Get on the subway. I got you, Okay," he said.

Maz was silent. Moments stretched over all the choices she could make, run to him, run away, run back home and kill her mom.

"I'll come." She hung up.

v v v

Dolores watched her daughter leave. Ashamed, she glanced nervously at her shoes, at the sliver of moon, at a neon-lit chimichanga food-truck with a line of people. Her neighbors avoided her eyes. A car throbbing with music drove by. She blinked as if waking up and climbed paint-blistered stairs to her apartment.

It was a wreck. A sofa was turned on its back. A lamp was knocked down, and its light cast the room in upside down shadows. Plates lay shattered on the floor. Wet food stains looked like wet graffiti on the wall. She sat down and winced, turned to find a large, shining kitchen knife under her butt.

Dolores sadly came to terms with the end. She faced it. Her daughter wanted to kill her. Her own flesh and blood. Satan got to her, making her sick like her grandmother. They both heard voices. All the time. Talk. To who? Crazy puta. I wish she'd tried to stab me. Go ahead piggy girl, my blood is your blood... puta, negra, bitch.

Dolores pounded the floor and kicked the air. And it came. A child-hood memory of being locked inside the closet. Her mother tried to hide her from the "voices" she heard too. It came at random. Her mom was humming a song and throwing laundry over a line. Her shadow on the billowing sheets, always made Dolores think of a theater show. The shadow would stop. And her mom fell and twisted into the sheet. She grabbed Dolores. Arm yanked like a rope. And threw her into the closet. Dolores kicked and punched the door. Her mom said the vampires were coming.

Inside the closet, her body was a clock—It was dinner time when her stomach gnawed. It was early evening when her legs ached to run. It was night when she peed and shit. Time melted. Dreams swirled in and out of the blackness.

Darkness swallowed Dolores. Silence peeled her apart until what remained was the rhythmic act of breathing and floating in a numb, timeless place. Her little puffs of exhale were enough to push her soul across the void. And then unexpectedly, the bolt was unlatched. The door opened, and her mom picked Dolores up, stroked her hair, and bathed her. Limp like a rag doll she was half awake, but after eating, a fury would surge in her like out-of-control fire. She would try to claw her mother's face, but the older woman gripped her wrists, and told her to calm down. They were safe from the vampires. Safe.

Dolores shook the memory out and opened her eyes. Her reflection was on the dark TV screen. How many decades since she left Puerto Rico. The cursed island? the cursed woman? Now she was a gaunt, old puta. The scratch on her cheek from where Maz punched her, burned a little. The apartment was quiet. Finally, it's over. No more craziness. No more "voices". No more.

"I'm safe. I'm safe." She staggered to her bedroom. Something banged. She turned, saw the window was open. Whatever. She waved tiredly and walked to the bedroom, closed the door.

The white curtains blew inward and wrapped around the form of a man, briefly, before untangling. A chair slid out of place. The door-beads split apart. The doorknob to the bedroom turned.

⌄ ⌄ ⌄

"Come on," Azmi commanded. Behind him Fadi, and Burger traded 'what the hell are we doing here' looks. The three tiptoed to the abandoned church.

"I've been here before." Azmi said. "Drug-heads camp out here, but they left. Maybe they left something behind."

Azmi was reckless. Always had been. He had gotten them into trouble their whole childhood, but each brush with danger left them with bigger stories to tell. It seemed worth it afterwards, but in the moment when your heart pounded in your chest...No, not so much.

The three boys bumped each other in the shadows, cursed, and shushed. They barely blinked, eyes sucked every particle of light until the last glow of the outside was gone and blackness drowned them. Using fingers on walls they felt their way. Down they went. Down into the cool abyss of the basement.

Azmi turned on his cellphone flashlight. He aimed its light that whizzed around on the floor. Footprints on dust, crisscrossed the hall. Burger and Fadi's shoes were visible next to him as he crouched to study the trail.

"What are you looking for?" Fadi nudged him with his knee. Azmi followed the footsteps. The circle of light made them seem as if they were floating in a void. They saw a dust covered incinerator and shuffled closer. The light rode over ash like a sun over miniature mountains. Fadi scooped some, it crunched in his hand. He held it under Azmi's phone, and saw finger bones.

"Oh shit. Oh shit. Oh shit!" He fell and scrambled. They collided into each other. The cellphone was on the floor, casting its beam up into the dark.

"Y-y-y-you saw it..." Azmi stammered. They panted like dogs. Inhale. Exhale. Inhale. Exhale.

"YOU SAW IT!" he yelled.

"Yes..."

"Me too..."

"Azmi," Burger said. "I want to leave."

"Okay. Okay," he swallowed. "Okay."

He aimed the phone forward. Its beam was a thin path in the blackness. Just ahead, the light showed long thin legs. So tall, up, up, up to bony hips high above their heads, then a cock and clitoris, a skeletal ribcage, faces moving under the skin that moaned in pain. Up, up, up to a head with insect eyes, twitching above a mouth of needle teeth. A tongue flickered like a fish flopping in the air.

Run. Run. Run. Blindly. Quickly. They ran up the stairs. One would beat down the other to jump ahead. They bounded two or three steps at a time. They huffed. They ran until legs and lungs burned. They ran until they should have reached outside.

Where was the fence? It wasn't this far; where was it? Where? Did they take a wrong turn? Did they go through another door? Was the monster still behind them?

Azmi wheezed. Femi helped Burger up the stairs. Cold sweat tingled on their bodies. A deep terror spiked in their minds.

"Keep going," Azmi husked. "Keep going."

They fought the pain in their feet. When their feet hurt too much, they crawled. How high could the stairs be? Burger counted the steps but kept losing track. Blinded by the dark, they touched walls to find a door, or boarded window. Nothing. Just smooth, damp rock and endless stairs.

They crawled without seeing, without hope. It had been more than hours, more than a whole night, more than could possibly exist in this church. The boys peed, and shit. They trod through the endless night, starving and dying of thirst.

At the abandoned church, police lights flashed. Cops saw their shadows loom on the walls like giant puppet.

"Ready?" one said.

"Ready."

Two went in. Flashlight beams crisscrossed the stairs. A putrid smell filled their noses. Pinching their nostrils, they touched the cobbled walls, and sparkling spider-webs. Clothing lay on the steps.

The flashlights rippled up a skeletal young man. He stared through milk white eyes. His cheeks were sunken. His lips chapped and raw.

They jumped back, and drew their weapons. He didn't move. His hands pulsed like weak flowers. They didn't know whether to cuff him or call for help.

One cop slid around, and up the young man. He was weak too. And sprawled on the steps. They yelled for an ambulance.

Downstairs the second squad explored the basement, and found ash on the floor. Their flashlights slashed through the dark. In the back was an incinerator. Inside were human bones.

You have been good to me.

The First One lifted crooked hands to the moon. It caressed the light. Flesh grew over bone. Intestinal gases steamed from splayed organs.

Come learn.

It made a beckoning motion to the waxing moon, and the Coven felt the call blaze their spines like Christmas lights. Men and women across the city jumped from windows. They leapt from rooftops. And vanished.

Countless shadows flowed like dark ink. A midnight river gushed along sidewalks, walls, and trains. Silhouettes paused under a light, danced a goofy two-step, and flew off. Profiles sped through the city. The telepathic web vibrated with laughter and shouts.

Across the world, the Coven felt the call. Each dove into a shadow

and traveled through its darkness and emerged in New York. Blackness was a portal like parting curtains between rooms. They followed the sweet call of the First One.

Shadows paused on a wall, arms raised, as if rising from bed. Or embraced on car seats, locked in a passionate kiss before racing off again. Or they shook like a churchgoer in ecstasy as people walked by.

Shadows gushed through alleys, trickled along the gutter, and flowed into the ruined church. Inside they materialized and landed on their feet. A naked throng huddled to hear the Word.

The First One teetered to them. It ran hands over its abdomen, where faces strained out against the skin. Shadows danced in a frenzy around its feet. It stooped down, scooped them up, and drank them. The veins in its neck throbbed.

Thirst. Thirst. Thirst.

The First One floated up, up, up. Shadows leapt, danced, fucked. The Coven physically present, swayed like mannequins on a rocking boat.

Let me show you.

The First One's skin became like glass.

We have been trapped here. Lost in their flesh. Forgetting ourselves.

On its body, a scene flickered of a man in the Oval Office. He unzipped a black satchel, and typed. Silos opened and missiles rose like angry stars. Chalk lines of exhaust were drawn across the sky. Nuclear explosions silently lit the earth. Ash fell like snow. The shadows fed on the pain and stepped on the land. They walked around smoking rubble, free, finally free of the thirst.

This man is our key. He will ignite the sky.

The First One vanished. Only its eyes remained, suspended like two coals in air. They evaporated. Footprints left a trail from the church. And went toward Manhattan.

"I've never given much thought to how I would die" Maz read out loud the first line of *Twilight*. She blinked, and snapped the book shut. It was painful.

The public library stank. Here was the emo-kid with laundry clip earrings. Here was the bum drooling as he slept. Here was the unkempt street scholar and notebook pages sprouting from shirt pockets.

Maz laughed bitterly. Lord, I am bored. She fiddled with her books. *Twilight, Vampires in History*, and *World Folktales*. If the voices weren't just her, then what the fuck were they? Not one goddam thing was helpful. This was all Hollywood and scared peasants. Virgin white girls trying to get laid. Boring.

Maz walked the stacks, and her fingertips trailed the books. If there was just a way of thinking about it all. She took a book off the shelf. It had a heavy musk. What a delicious smell. Age. Wisdom. Loneliness.

"Capital is dead labour which, vampire like, lives only by sucking living labor, and lives the more, the more labour it sucks." The line zinged her. Who was this? Karl Marx. He was an economist? Did he hear them too? She kept reading.

*I try and try
not to think
about
the wall.*

Six

"I'M GOING TO WIN THIS MOTHER FUCKER."

Ronald Balk sprayed holding gel. He picked, fluffed, combed and fussed his hair. Perfect. "Mr. Future President."

"You look like a movie star." Harold Roter, the body-man theatrically bowed.

"So damn thirsty!" Balk rubbed his throat.

"I'll get water," Roter went to the next room. The lights were off. He didn't turn them on. On the wall his shadow peeled free, like a silhouette becoming a 3-D image. Dark hands lifted a cup, and pinched a black drop from its finger. It blossomed like a dark rose in the water. Roter brought it to Balk, who downed it in a quick gulp.

Slapping his hands, Balk joined his wife Melavia and they descended the escalator. She didn't touch him and stayed to the side. He flew into a fury if the cameras were not on him. It was his presidential campaign launch. Half advertising stunt, half protest against the decline of America; he puffed his chest like corporate warrior. But why was he so damn thirsty?

After his daughter introduced him, Balk bounded to the podium to bask in the magnifying glass of the media. He felt alive. And sharp. A humming at the base of his neck, crystalized the room. Adrenaline? Whatever it was, the crowd were easy to read. Every face had a loose thread that if you pulled, their raw selves would spill out into the open.

"There's been no fans like my fans." He stoked their fears with words. Balk knew his people. They feared losing what little they had to strangers. Drawing up the nightmares they choked down, he conjured up images of rapist, criminal Mexicans crossing into America as it slid into Third World status. The mood in the room and in the millions of rooms he was being projected into, was combustible. How am I doing this? How do I get to be so good at everything I do?

"Maz? Maz? Yo, where'd you go?" Jesus spat into his phone. "This is like the eightieth message. Call me. Are you coming? Where are you?"

He waited all night for her. And woke up with the phone in his hand. On the subway and at school, the silence weighed heavy. The day was like a held breath that he wanted to exhale into an angry 'where-the-hell-have-you-been' question. But she never called.

Jesus asked her friends. They didn't know. Some fucking friends, he snarled. He cornered her pill buyers. They were calling her too. Like him, no response. Did he have any of her pills? *No*, he shook his head, *no*.

Leaving school, he saw police cars. Cops stood in a grim line.

They seemed to look not at the students but at the streets. Why is Five-O here?

He looked at his phone again. Nothing. Nothing for a long time, now.

"I understand Maz," Jesus muttered.

Someone called him. His short, bulldog-shaped father Miguel, stood next to his lanky, younger brother Batista. They waved him over to the family van.

"Hurry," his father yelled. And hugged him hard.

"What's up?" Jesus squirmed free. "Why you all MMA on me?"

"You're not going to school tomorrow." Miguel opened the van door. "Whole bunch of people..." He snapped his fingers. "Gone."

"Pops people vanish all the time." Jesus leaned back in the car seat and scrolled through his phone. Headlines read, "MORE MISSING! FAMILIES GRIEVE FOR THE LOST!" Each new site blared the same dire warning. Interviews with sad, wobbly-voiced New Yorkers filled the screen. What the hell? Everyone was freaking out.

True to form, his boys sent texts celebrating the craziness. Raffi even asked to get more Head Floaters. It was the nick-name for Maz's pills. He told him no, she'd disappeared too.

Oh no. Sorry.

Nigga you ain't sorry. Fuck outta here with all that.

Miguel turned up the radio to hear Balk, the TV real estate guy with the ugly comb-over that looked like a rooster had died on his head. Jesus thought he was full of shit.

"We need to build walls. Tall walls. To stop them from coming in," Balk shouted. "And clean house. Get the criminals back behind bars. The Democrats want to let them loose. Tell me is that justice? Is it?"

His father and brother were hypnotized. They nodded to the beat of Balk's voice like birds pecking at bread crumbs.

"See Jesus." Miguel jabbed the air with a forefinger. "This man

speaks truth. Watch him. He will be the next president."

Jesus rolled his eyes. His father cranked up the volume.

"These scum break into our homes," Balk lowered his tone to a dark warning. "They rape our women, steal our jobs, and kill!"

"Pops, why you listening to this Hitler?" Jesus shouted over the radio. "You act like he wants your spic ass in the country. We learned about this in school. It's called fascism."

In the rearview mirror, his father glanced at Batista. The two laughed like jackals. Batista turned and gave the Nazi salute. He flipped his hand around and gave Jesus the middle finger.

"See that finger? That's how big your dick is," Jesus clowned. "It's a birth defect. Guess you take after Pops."

Miguel told them to shut up. Jesus sat back and looked out of the window. Two cops ran to join two other officers wrestling someone on the street. They tossed the man like a big, dirty rag doll. It was Picasso. The word "thirst" was scrawled in chalk above them. Picasso barked and snapped his jaws. A cop aimed his gun at him. Jesus pressed his face to the window. His father drove away.

New York was in a panic. Tabloids showed the missing Down Syndrome child, Consuela, and an attorney who vanished in Central Park. Eight million people lived here. Each day some were shot, mugged, raped or killed. Who didn't know someone, who knew someone, who was aced? The casual, anonymous violence stirred fear. It was as ignitable as gas. All it took was one graphic story to ignite it. And here it was. People had been abducted, and their faces were on TV screens looking down on New York like a host of missing angels.

Paranoia spewed like a thick, sulfurous fog. It hissed from every face and every quick corner chat. It was a relentless fear that each New

Yorker inhaled, making them hallucinate their own nightmares. Parents walked children everywhere. Young women peered down alleys where newspapers blew in circles. The elderly bolted doors.

Jesus walked to the bodega and saw blurred faces in the window watching the street. None of this felt right. None of this fit.

Butt-Butt, Sam and Trey turned the corner. They were round the way guys from Louis Armstrong projects. He waved. They waved. They fist bumped, slapped hands, and half hugged like a ghetto version of the Three Stooges. Jesus squinted at the American flag on their shirts, swaying like a single red, white and blue ribbon across their chests.

"You feeling this?" Jesus pointed to their shirts.

Sam stretched his shirt out like a trampoline.

"Yeah, we taking America back." Trey stuck his chest out. "Tired of these fucking aliens, fucking our shit up."

Butt-Butt mirrored what Trey did. He puffed himself up too. Jesus choked down laughter.

"We're the Safety Militia." Trey gestured to the street like an orchestra conductor. "Long Island pigs don't know the hood. They just get in the way. We doing the right thing, letting everyone know they can count us for a change, you know wha' I'm saying? Step up the game, taking care of the community."

Jesus asked Sam with his eyes *If he was down with this Seal Team Six bullshit*. Sam was a little retarded. He followed anyone with a big voice. It got him a scar on his neck. Trey enlisted him into a turf fight Sam had no business in. Trey was a hot head. He had been trying to carve his name in Brooklyn since childhood. Fatherless like most of the boys here, but he tried to make up for it with fame.

Jesus told them 'Good Luck', nodded, and peaced-out. In the bodega was an American flag on the window. A man leaned over the counter, jabbing a finger at Muhammed.

"Don't think we ain't watching you." He grabbed his bag and left. Muhammed slammed the drawer shut. His eyes were bright and hot.

"You okay?" Jesus asked.

"Just a stupid motherfucker." Muhammed's jaw clenched. "Thinks I don't belong here."

˅ ˅ ˅

"Another one," Balk shook the New York Post. "Another one missing."

"Life in the city." Roter brought a cup of water.

Balk drank to wet his oddly-dry throat. It felt like sandpaper. He waved the aides in, and in a minute, they made a glowing circle of I-Pads and cellphones. Together they marched to the TV studio, a loud yammering of polls and soundbites. He zoned them out.

Balk walked to the podium. Cameras flashed in a string of strobe lights. He knew the media saw him as a joke, a buffoon. He knew they hated him.

The humming at the base of his neck returned. A strange euphoria sharpened his senses. He heard voices inside voices, like wearing headphones that played two different stations. He looked at the reporters. Thoughts were audible. They had professional poker faces, but their internal streams of consciousness filled the room. Balk leaned in.

They were scared. The liberal media. When he spoke, they shook because they buried, inside themselves, fears of stigma or exile. Inside them, memories churned at being told they weren't American enough, or they were bullied. Balk focused on a black reporter and heard a child crying on a playground. He studied a Spanish reporter with nice legs and saw a teen, trembling, as police joked about her being a wetback. Another cameraman was once beaten to red pulp, for being caught sucking a kid's dick.

He read them. And how easily there were cowed. They would turn

to jelly. All he had to say to scare them, to shake them to their core, was *"GET THE HELL OUT!"*

v v v

Jesus watched Balk rant on TV. His family was on the couch, greedily slurping up dinner and following every word. Even Mom nodded approvingly. He felt like an alien.

"Don't let the liberals fool you. Oh, the refugees need a place to stay." On TV, he pumped a fist. "But they are snakes. You can't change the nature of a snake!"

Balk created an angry world, in which they were the last line of defense against every enemy you could name—illegal immigrants, terrorists, and perverts. Ugly smiles crept up on his family's faces when Balk dissed a disabled journalist. They slapped their knees. Jesus put his spoon down, wondering what was happening.

When did his family cross the line? Did it begin with the Down Syndrome kid vanishing? But disappearances were a sad fact of city life. Somehow Balk tapped into the tribal mind of the city. After 9/11, a simmering hate bubbled like oil beneath the surface. Now he dropped the face of each vanished New Yorker into it like a lit match. It was common to see burned Mexican flags, or shredded pages of the Koran taped to windows of Yemini bodegas. Or "USA" scribbled in magic marker on subway posers.

Jesus began to see Balk's face on shirts, jackets, and the bags people used to carry their groceries home. He didn't notice because he was in the bubble of crazy that Maz blew around herself, even though he had only briefly been inside it. But when she cut him off, he was left blinking in a New York that had changed into an eight-million person street mob, foaming at the mouth for justice against an enemy they couldn't find.

Miguel and Batista cheered Balk on. Jesus shook his head. They must have been hurt for a long time. Maybe it had been smothered under vulgar jokes and long hours at work. Truth is they felt small, and Balk made them feel big.

"Mom what you think?" Jesus prodded.

"I just hope he can get things straightened out." She wiped the table clean. "We can't live scared in our own city."

She handed Miguel and Batista cold Presidente beer. They thanked her without looking up.

"Go to your windows! Let them know!" Balk left the podium. "GET THE HELL OUT! GET THE HELL OUT!"

Jesus palmed his eyes. *Wow he's lost it. I am watching the end of his campaign.* A charged silence filled the room as Balk strode to the windows and shouted the slogan. He was almost sad for his father and brother, who had hoped this New York tycoon could redeem their hard lives.

"Get the hell out my country!" The shout came from outside like a gunshot.

The family squeezed their heads out of the window. Neighbors stood on rusty fire escapes and hollered.

"Get the hell out my country...terrorists!"

Mom banged pots. Jesus's blood turned cold. His brother climbed onto the fire escape and screamed along. And his father too. Rage burst into night like fireworks. On TV, Balk smiled and threw his arms up in triumph into the night like fireworks.

On the train, Jesus quickly breathed in and out. Wall Street men wore 'Balk for President' pins and made ugly jokes. The air was sour. 'Balk for President' advertisements glowed above his head. *Damn it!* The guy was everywhere.

He got off the train, bounded up the stairs, and once outside, saw Picasso's chalk figures. A crate, broken bottles, and newspapers were scattered around like a dirty nest. *Maybe the police locked him up?*

Jesus sat on the crate, leaning back to watch clouds unspool across the sky. The sun left orange blobs under his eyelids. He dozed off.

He awoke with a spasm. Wallet? Cellphone? Okay. Okay. He looked around and saw that Picasso had drawn a crown with a radio tower above it. Radio signals written in white chalk on the brick pointed to another subway station. A cartoon building at the end had a stick figure of a woman leaning form a window, fanning flames.

"SHE SLEEPS HERE."

Picasso had given him directions to Maz.

"Thank you, old man." Jesus slapped the wall.

Where was she? He followed Picasso's directions to East New York. And he hated East New York.

Jesus sat on a stoop. Half a block down, homeless men rolled on the ground. One had long, gooey streams of spit draped on his mouth.

"Oh fuck me!" Jesus grimaced.

It was a carnival of urban pathology. Junkies floated by in closed-eyed bliss. They stumbled over garbage cans and cried.

"FIRE! FIRE IN THE HOLE!" a woman yelled. On the fourth floor, she thrust a leg out of the window and did a lurid dance.

"Fire in the hole?" Jesus remembered Picasso's image. Flames. Window. A woman. He ran to the building, wiggled through a door hanging by a chain. Inside the dead brownstone, the air was cool and fetid.

He followed a trail of water bottles, food wrappers, and condoms. A Pez dispenser lay in the dirt.

"Maz!" he yelled.

A bottle rolled by his feet.

"MAZ?"

A door slammed. He ran, turned a corner, and saw where she slept. On the floor were cans of Chef Boyardee. On the wall, a map of the city was taped with a purple crayon 'X' marked near Wall Street and City Hall.

"Why are you running?" Jesus squatted down, picked through the trash. "What are you running from?"

NEED MONEY TO EAT.

Maz placed the cardboard sign at her feet. Wall Street business men and women flowed by yelling numbers into cellphones. Where were the vampires? In the map she made, they huddled near power. Banks. Police stations. City Halls. State Houses. Military bases.

Thirst. Thirst. Thirst.

Pain clanged inside like a heavy bell. Maz chewed her lower lip raw. One was coming. And she held the cardboard sign like a shield.

Thirst. Thirst. Thirst.

Maz clutched her throat. The moist lining was bone dry. She gulped water. Her head swayed as a man strutted by. He had on a purple, silk tie, and Gucci suit.

Thirst. Thirst. Thirst.

Thought shattered. He trotted into the New York Stock Exchange. The pain ebbed to a low tide of broken glass scraping her skull. She unclenched her fingers from the sign.

"Jesus." She wiped sweat from her forehead. "That put some hairs on my chest."

Over the pillars of the NYSE, a large American flag billowed. More vampires entered and more aching throbs pulsed as each one walked by

her. Breathing slow, she saw that her palm had a ring of fingernail prints.

Maz turned over the cardboard, and it said "THEY'RE HERE." Raising it up, she pushed into the crowd flowing down the street.

"Do you know they're here?" she asked passers-by. "Can you feel them? Want to see who they are? I'll show you."

Bored New Yorkers shoulder-bumped Maz like a pinball from one person to another. She pushed back and held the sign.

"Does anyone want to know the truth?" she asked.

Maz dragged herself up the street. The cardboard sign bumped against her leg. She walked past drug dealers who leaned on cars.
"It's a beautiful day in the neighborhood," Maz sang under her breath. "Won't you be mine? "

A bushy-haired man trotted next to her. He twitched as if being shocked by a battery.

"Hey, hey, can we play, we play again?"

"Oh Mumbles!" Maz shook her head.

"Please, please play 9/11." he skipped, sniffed, rolled his eyes, scratched his beard, and made a flying motion with his hands.

"Okay, okay." Maz pulled out paper and folded it into an airplane. "Here we go Mumbles. It's 9/11. Can you stop the terrorists?"

She threw the paper airplane. It sailed over his head, and he chased it.

"Catch the terrorists!" Maz hollered.

The paper airplane fell on a car and one of the drug dealers threw it again. Wherever it landed, someone picked it up, and launched it. The guys on the street loved seeing Mumbles run around chasing 9/11.

Maz ducked into the abandoned building. Legs felt like a sack of bricks. A heavy fatigue crushed her. Questions spun around but no answers. The vampires were in charge. They are invisible. And if they discovered her, they'd kill her.

When she got to her makeshift room, Jesus was there. Maz jumped. His face simmered with anger, sadness, curiosity, and hope.

"Maz." he pointed at her map on the wall. "What's this? What's going on?"

"O.P.P." She giggled. "You know me."

"What?"

"Other People's Pain," she mumbled. "It was a hit single in the 90's. Don't you watch VH-1?"

"Maz..."

"Oh, don't Maz me!" she snarled. "Don't use that therapy session voice. Your Maz isn't here anymore. She's was a girl trapped inside a blue pill. Blue this. Blue that. Blue is the color of her favorite snack."

She paced back and forth.

"Blue was numbness," she began a manic monologue. "Blue was blindness. Blue was no touch me. Now I am here. It is loud here and thirsty. And I'm the only one who knows the truth. We're being eaten by vampires!"

"Maz..." Jesus said.

"Don't know who you're talking about." she rolled her eyes, splayed her hands in mock innocence.

"Maz please..." Jesus opened his bag. "You need help."

"La la la la la." she fingered her ears.

"I brought your pills." He handed her a bottle. "Please come back."

She stopped. Eyes focused on the bottle. She plucked it out of his palm. The date on the label was old.

"Maz, they paid me to steal it from your locker," he said.

"Paid you," her voice was a whispery puff. Her head tilted as if trying to roll the words into place. Her lips tightened. Tears streamed down.

"Paid you," she said.

"I'm so sorry," Jesus stepped forward.

"Paid you. Paid you. Paid you. Paid you." Her hands trembled.

"Hey, hey," Jesus tried to grab hold of her.

Batting his hands away, Maz screamed. They wrestled. Blind with tears, she struck him, and ran. He tackled her to the floor.

"Why..." she whined.

"I'm sorry. I'm sorry. I'm sorry." Jesus's arms locked Maz down as she thrashed.

"Why?" she said over and over. Exhausted from the struggle, Maz was too spent to make a sound. But she kept asking. Her mouth moving silently.

"Why?"

∨ ∨ ∨

When Maz fell asleep, Jesus lay next her. He hoped they could work it out. Maybe she could forgive him?

"Swallow this."

He woke up. Maz straddled him like a boulder. Knees pinched his arms. He kicked to get leverage. Damn girl was too heavy.

"Swallow!" she said.

Maz pushed a pill through his lips. He spat it out.

"Get the fuck off me!" he barked.

"Want to see me again," she asked. "Then eat this. Or you will never see me."

A holy fever glowed around her face.

"You took these pills from me," she sneered. "You watched them carry me out on a gurney. And you did it for money. Now you come back

to rescue me? No. No. No. You don't get absolution that fucking easy."

Jesus stopped squirming. He wanted to say two wrongs don't make a right. Or yank her down by the hair and run from this disgusting, homeless female. Not knowing why, he opened his mouth.

"That's a good boy." She smiled icily. "Blessed are the meek for they shall inherit the Earth."

She placed two pills on his tongue. He swallowed. When she stood, knots of pain ebbed on his arms.

"They'll kick in soon," Maz said over her shoulder. "Try not to throw up too much. I sleep here."

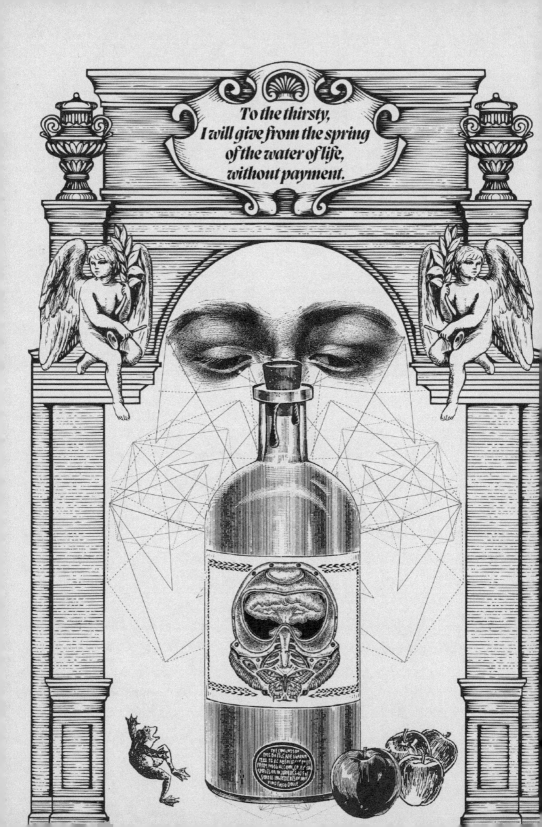

To the thirsty,
I will give from the spring
of the water of life,
without payment.

Seven

"WELL FOLKS, THEY FOUND THE SCUMBAGS,"

Balk thrust The New York Post into the air. "Azmi. Fadi. Burger. Muslims. All of them."

The stadium shook as thousands booed. Curses rained down. *Kill the ragheads. Kill the sand-niggers.* Rage rose into the air like a giant, vaporous serpent that snapped at the newspaper Balk shook above the podium.

"Innocent human beings, kidnapped by jihadists." He pointed at the headline. "And taken to an abandoned church where they burned to ash! These are sick people. Three Muslim teens. How many more of these terrorists do we let into the country?"

In the front row, fans leaned forward like shark teeth. American flags were waved. A woman in red, white and blue face paint tore off her shirt. "BUILD THE WALL! BUILD THE WALL! BUILD THE WALL." They chanted.

"Damn right!" Balk raised his arms.

Stage lights crisscrossed the crowd and highlighted random faces like mini portraits. One light showed a man baring his canines. The child on his shoulders bared his too. Another light showed three friends ripping a Koran to pieces.

At the podium, Balk gazed lovingly at the near riot in the stadium. And then a flash blinded him. Was it a camera? Orange spots floated in his vision.

Rubbing his eyes, he heard a vast silence. He blinked and could see again. Every person had been transformed into a statue of dust. It was like a nightmare-mannequin store. The father with a child on his shoulders. Dust. The friends tearing at the Koran. Dust.

Balk felt wind blow into the stadium. The dust figurines crumbled. Heads fell and split on the floor. Clothes tumbled away like rags. The grains stung him. The storm churned into a dark, yellow fury.

Balk blinked again. The sound of the crowd rushed back. Fans shook signs. Fans yelled his name. Slowly he peeled his hands from the podium. Dark sweat-prints stained the wood. Quickly he waved and walked off stage.

Balk reached for his throat. *Water. I need water.* He motioned for something to drink. Roter gave him a bottle. Balk swigged it sloppily. And palmed his forehead.

Thirst. Thirst. Thirst.

˅ ˅ ˅

Am I going crazy? What the fuck happened up there?

Balk rubbed his temples. The vision he had at during the stadium rally terrified him. Is it a medical condition? Was he going crazy?

The private jet coasted on the clouds like a boat. Balk looked through the window at the sky. The cell phone buzzed, but he ignored it. He couldn't let himself lose it now. The presidency was at his fingertips.

He tried to swallow, but the saliva scraped a dry throat. *Goddamn it! Not again.* He got up, and sway-walked between the seats to the kitchen. *Why am I so goddamn thirsty? What the hell. Feel like I could drink a lake.*

Balk bent to the faucet, and gurgled water from the sink. Liquid vanished into his mouth. His throat felt like sand. Balk staggered to the bedroom. The bright ovals of the plane windows stung his eyes. He ripped off his tie and dropped on the bed.

"Help…" he husked. "Help!"

He twisted the sheets. Skin tightened like shrink wrap. Eyes scratched like marbles. Hair cracked apart like brittle spaghetti. *Oh God! Oh God!*

"It's not God," said Roter.

Balk saw him on the bed, and the shadow against the wall slipped free. It rippled over the sheets, and its dark hand lifted up. Roter cut the shadow's hand with a knife, and black liquid fell drop by drop.

"God doesn't exist." He caressed Balk.

Balk whipped his head.

"Stop!" Roter scolded. "Stop." He thumbed Balk's mouth and pried the lips open. The blood of the shadow squirmed like maggot larva over the teeth.

"Drink."

Wild sweetness tingled in Balk's mouth. He stopped fighting and sucked the black thumb like a popsicle.

"Good boy." Roter squeezed harder. "Good boy."

Shadows
descend and

move forward,
smelling of
SWEAT
and blood.

Eight

"OKAY SLEEPING BEAUTY." Maz kicked Jesus. "Time to wake up."

He groggily rolled over. Vomit caked his mouth. Maz roughly washed him with a damp washcloth. He flailed and pushed.

Maz cackled. "Look at him. Baby isn't feeling good."

Jesus palmed his head. *What the hell was going on? Why am I even here? What did she do to me?*

Maz chiseled the vomit off with a fingernail and kissed him.

"You have a Knight-In-Shining-Armor complex," she said. "You want to save me." And batted her eyelashes like a 1930's Hollywood starlet. "I want to save me too." She blew a kiss at him. "But it's too late. I've seen things, and the only way for you to save me, is if you see them too...Capeesh?"

Jesus squinted. Sunlight was like a nail pounded into his eyes. The pills he stole from her locker were on the floor. She didn't take them.

Why bother? Why try to be sane anymore. He picked up and swallowed one. Maz kissed him deeply, sucked his tongue and spat out the pill.

"No." She cupped his face. "I need you here."

∨ ∨ ∨

Maz wiped her underarms with baby Wet Naps. Jesus did too. Naked at the window, they dried themselves in sunbeams. After they dressed, she put on earmuffs to muffle the "voices". They were going to find a vampire.

On the subway, Jesus felt New York change. Its loud bang, clash, boom, yelling, honking, cursing, selling, begging, laughing, and grunting had previously comforted him. Now, he flinched at noise. Maz covered his ears as they rode the train to Wall Street.

Outside they ran past the iconic metal bull and slapped its ass. Maz was jumpy. Her head swiveled left and right. Jesus did not see a thing.

"Where I'm taking you," she said. "There's a lot of them. Try not to scream when you see them, okay, don't announce us to the vamps. Last thing I need is to be disappeared, when I'm this close." She pinched her fingers close together.

"Vampires!" Jesus said in a numb voice.

"Yes," Maz said. "The undead, the blood suckers, the eternal watchers, the ones who don't take holy water showers, who hate garlic, you know...vampires."

"Like Twilight?" he asked.

"Like Twilight." She slapped her knees. "Yes, like Twilight. Exactly. Like I want to fuck a vampire but cock-tease a werewolf because it's hot to have them fight over me, I am Helen to the Ancient War between vampires and werewolves, all played by sexy, white teens snarling and speaking good, college, thespian English. Yes, I'll have a vampire's baby because they can go all night, Yes, you moron, this is Twilight."

Maz spread her arms and spun theatrically. "I am Bella, hoe of the undead." She leaned in and whispered, "I know what vampire semen tastes like."

Jesus shrank away. "What does it taste like Maz?"

"Kiss me and find out."

He shook his head. "I can't with you."

Maz grabbed his sleeve. "Come on! We'll see one." She took out her cellphone, and pointed at the other side of the street.

"Look," she husked.

He did. He waited. He waited longer. A restaurant worker took a smoke break. Delivery men unloaded boxes. Business execs typed on cell phones.

"See it?" She nudged him. "See it?"

Jesus shrugged.

"The shadow in the middle," she said.

Jesus focused on the shadows moving against the wall. One was oddly tall. He rolled his eyes. Well goodbye to my self-respect. It's gone. I vomited it up with the pills.

The restaurant worker and delivery man left. Seconds slowly ticked by. Jesus got bored. He saw the tall shadow. No one was on the sidewalk. Jesus shook his head like a swimmer clearing water from his ears. He looked again. The shadow climbed over the doorframe and crawled back inside. He leapt back.

"Ooh," Jesus covered his mouth. "Ooh."

"Do you need to scream?" She gently took his head. "Bring it in. Bring it in."

He bit her coat sleeve.

"Oh my God!" Jesus clutched Maz. "Oh my God."

ᴠ ᴠ ᴠ

On a bench at Chelsea Piers, Maz showed Jesus photos of vampire shadows. He leaned over the cellphone as she scrolled. In one image, two shadows danced over a crashed car in Midtown. In another, one choked a baby.

"I'm sorry." Jesus gave the phone back. "A lot of times, in my head, I said you were crazy. Cute but crazy." His hands trembled. "Why do you call them vampires?"

"I had a crush on Kiefer Sutherland in *The Lost Boys*." Maz blew steam off her cup of tea. "You know what it is? In the movies, vampires always want blood. Well, I feel how thirsty they are. They drain anything, anyone they can. It's like, like." Motioning a hand to her mouth. "They thirst for something inside us."

She sipped the tea and looked at her wobbly reflection in the cup. They sat in silence. The ocean sloshed grey waves. The tourists that walked by seemed on the other side of a one-way mirror.

"I don't blame you for thinking I was crazy." Maz put an arm around Jesus. "I thought I was crazy too. A schizo. Nothing to no one. But I was wrong. I could just hear them. But like which is worse? Being schizo or hearing vampires?"

"Oh hell," Jesus joked. "Vampires? Give me schizophrenia any day—Fucking vampires?

She mugged him, and he playfully bit her fingers. They lay on the bench and entwined their legs.

"So what do we do?" he asked.

"Move," Maz said

"Anywhere safe?" Jesus tenderly stroked her neck.

"No," she said. "Nowhere is safe." Straightening up, Maz looked at the ocean. "I took you to Wall Street for a reason. They love power. They use it to hide. Lately they have been noisy. They go through phases. When the moon is full, it's a like a Pride March. Loud. Happy. But when it's thin. They are silent. And desperate."

"So what do we do?" Jesus sat up. "We can't run. We can't fight them."

"Actually." Maz threw the cup. "We can but it means doing something you won't like."

He scrunched his eyes.

Nine

"REMEMBER THOSE LONELY AFTERNOONS when your father was working?" Roter kissed Balk on the forehead like a child. "You heard music coming from the sky. You thought it was God. It was us. We were calling you. Your mother forced you to take medicine. The music left. You were so sad. We missed you."

"Me?" Balk smiled in wonder. His head was in Roter's lap. They lay on the floor, in front of the window that overlooked New York.

"Yes, you." Roter stroked his cheek. "The End Times are now. We want you to come with us. Do you want to join us?"

"Yes," Balk whispered. He opened his mouth, and shadows crawled inside him.

ᕙ ᕙ ᕙ

The First One spread his arms wide to the moon. Tongue flickering like an eel, it licked the pale light that brushed skin. The eldest vampire rubbed the length of its body, as if erasing itself. Patches vanished. And then a fading glitter.

Its shadow rippled under the church fence and down the street. It poured over pavement, up walls, and rooftops. It oozed down to a homeless man. A tall shadow stroked him with long sharp fingers. The man's skin became leathery. Mouth puckered like a prune. He crumbled to dust. The shadow flowed beneath cars, puddled around the boots of police who guarded Balk Tower. The protestors waved signs. They jutted middle fingers and saw themselves in the reflective helmets of the cops.

It flew up the elevator shaft and thinned into the crease of the carpet. The doorknob turned, and The First One's shadow wrapped itself around Balk, who lay panting on the floor. His eyes rolled back.

We have loved you for so long.

"You have?" Balk was pale. Veins pulsed under his skin like blue snakes.

Do you want to live forever?

Hope. Grief. Joy. Balk bobbed on giant waves that broke from his heart. The man sank into childhood.

"Yes. Please. Take me with you." He entwined his hands with the shadow.

Can you leave this world behind?

"Yes, I can."

Then destroy this world. Nothing can be done for the others. But you will be anointed.

Balk saw a vision of nuclear missiles silently flash over cities. Skeletons were visible like a macabre dance before they were swept up in a mushroom cloud. Balk caressed the blinding explosion. Why not—what was this world anyway? Lies, and liars. Thieves. Hatred. Maggots biting maggots. Why him though? What made him special? What did they get out of this?

You doubt us.

"Why me?"

The shadow's hands embraced Balk and a web of throbbing voices, the Coven, wove themselves around him. He saw through their eyes. They pulled his vison from his office and building, beyond the city and above the sky. They hurled him to a distant bright place that was their home. He was to be brought there and given a place among them. The most powerful presences, the oldest ones would inspect him at first like a strange trophy.

"You need me."

We do. We must prove our long absence was worth it. And that a world has been cleansed for the others.

"And I will live forever?"

Yes. Forever.

He heard through their ears. And felt through their skin. In the blur a few faces came into focus. Many were from the very elite moguls he signed property and entertainment deals with across the decades.

Balk opened his eyes. The office was dark. Roter was gone. The First One was gone. His cellphone blinked with unanswered calls. On shaky legs, he went to the window. New York City was a giant maze. He studied the traffic that looked like toy cars, small enough that he could reach down and pick one up.

"Yes, it is time to end all this."

⌄ ⌄ ⌄

The First One melted into the dark. He left Balk at the window, his spine had been transformed into a hot antenna for the Coven. Now it was time to rest.

It entered the shadows in the office and emerged in the shadows in the basement. Humid air sat heavy in the room. The low time was here. The physical body had to atrophy again, until the waxing moon lifted them up.

Children I must sleep.

They screamed. The Coven sensed The First One's soothing pulse recede. Soon they could not fly or even remember. All they would know was thirst. They thrashed in their host bodies like birds in a cage.

The more powerful kept shreds of memory. A faint tether bound their minds to the first days. The weaker ones hunted like sharks through the city. Dumb and bestial they were careless. Prowling alleys, rehab centers and homeless camps, the lower-order vampires left piles of dust in the morning. Sometimes people saw them. And when spotted, the Coven punished them. But not without sympathy. Deep hate drove them too. Living inside human flesh, was like being buried alive. The branches of nerves and blood vessels coiled around their ephemeral beings, like barbed wire. Freedom, they thirsted freedom.

Soon my children. Soon.

⌄ ⌄ ⌄

"I'm on my period," Maz said.

"I don't care." Jesus lowered his face between her thighs. "Like tomato soup down here."

She play-kicked him, but felt his tongue on her clit. Pleasure

warmed her. She relaxed. Jesus ate rhythmically as she grunted.

"Wait. Wait. Let me see you."

He looked up. Nose, mouth and chin were red. Maz laughed. "You look like Braveheart."

"Free-ee-ed-o-m," he whispered. She pushed him back down. A crack opened in her heart. Love wrapped itself around him. She loved this stupid, crazy guy.

⌄ ⌄ ⌄

Voices woke Jesus. Wiping his face, he looked around. The bedroom was a dark blue ocean. Maz snored next to him.

Thirst. Thirst. Thirst.

Panic zapped him awake. He swiveled out of bed, got up, and grabbed the bat he kept in the corner. Heart kicking, he was ready to swing. He stood over Maz, welding the bat.

Thirst. Thirst. Thirst.

Lips blistered. Throat felt like a desert. They were close. After five, painful swallows, spit coated his gums again.

⌄ ⌄ ⌄

"I am New York's hardest-working cab driver." Diego checked his reflection in the rearview mirror. The bags under his eyes were as big as purses.

Yep, he thought. *Look at Mr. Old Man Driver going nowhere fast. Time to rest. No more money to be made tonight.*

On the windshield, a handprint appeared. More covered the car like a cave painting. The back door opened. Cold air woke Diego, and he scrambled to shut it. Cursing, he got back in and saw a woman in the backseat.

"Lady..." he began.

She gave him a twenty. Diego started the car. He glanced in the rear-view mirror. She was gone. He spun around. Sharp teeth tore him. The steering wheel spun. The car jumped the curb. People threw bags and scattered. Diego clawed the door handle but his fingers broke into dust. The whole arm collapsed into powder. He burst into clouds that filled the taxi.

Diego's head rolled on the seat. *Why? why? why?* She picked it up and squeezed. His thoughts blew apart into darkness.

A crowd circled the taxi and watched a woman flee the vehicle. Beige dust blew out. They called after her. *Miss! Miss! You okay? You hurt?*

One of the bystanders, cautiously looked inside. Silt-like powder coated the dashboard. The hazard lights blinked on and off.

"Bystanders say a woman ran out," The reporter stooped into the taxi and scooped up a handful dust.

Thirst. Thirst. Thirst.

The TV shut off. The woman paced the apartment back and forth. The comforting hum of voices from the Coven stopped. The silence pressed down like a warning. She nervously picked at her cuticles.

On the wall, shadows reached for her. Yanked across the room, she clawed the carpet. The thin, crooked fingers like vines, entwined around her ankles. They hauled her out to the patio. She wrestled them, but more shadows came like hellish imps holding her down. The blue sky was split by the sunrise.

No. No. No.

Smoke puffed from her eye sockets. Writhing, she cooked, bubbled, boiled. Hands caught fire. Face caught fire. A huge flame erupted over her body as she spun. Ash blew across the sky.

Maz and Jesus held hands on the subway. The underground graffiti whizzed by like a dingy art museum.

"Let's get the last of your shit," he said. "Live with me until we figure it out."

Maz breathed Lamaze style. Maybe a new version of herself would pop out of all this horror? Jesus loved her. When he touched her it felt like cement poured into her broken places. She felt strong. Maybe now she could let her mother go.

Maz felt an old hope that her mother missed her. Would she rush to Maz with open arms and apologize? Where did these fantasies come from? She knew the Bitch wouldn't open the door. But still the old hope.

Jesus guided her out of the subway, and when they turned the corner three NYPD cars were in front of the building. Two officers, one short Latino, one tall and Black, pointed at them. The Black officer beckoned with his hands.

"Maz Ramos?" he said.

Maz was there but not there. The sound of their voices was turned down. Police circled them, badges like bright stars. Their eyes peeled Jesus and Maz to find guilt or innocence. They said Dolores was missing. Her mother was missing. Did Maz know where she had gone? Where had Maz been?

They got her. Maz knew it, in the way you just know. The vampires got her. And she would never be found. Throwing her head back she screamed. Her legs collapsed. Jesus and the cops held her. She screamed, and screamed, and screamed.

An ambulance came. Paramedics unfolded a gurney. An EMT checked her pulse and gave her an oxygen mask. Maz lay on the gurney and watched the lights paint the street red and green, as if it were Christmas. A stethoscope was pressed to her chest. A needled pricked her arm. Ice filled her head.

I came to see the wreck.
I came to see the damage that was done and the treasures that prevail.

Ten

TWO BLURRY FIGURES SAT ON THE HOSPITAL BED WITH MAZ.

One was Consuela who rubbed a hole in her throat. The other was veiled in shadows.

"You came back for me?" Maz husked. "You said you couldn't stay."

She asked me to bring her to you. We have to take you the beginning.

The other woman stepped into the light. It was Dolores. She rubbed Maz's chest like when she had the flu.

"Mom," she asked. "Why did you hate me so much?"

Come.

Wobbly and weak, Maz hung like a rag doll in their arms. They half-dragged her past the emergency room unit and the dark hallways. The further she walked, the more the linoleum became moist soil. Twigs bit into her feet.

They were always with us.

The full moon glowed like a pearl. Maz saw her family's old house in Puerto Rico. The cement walls were painted like a coral reef, and white chickens slept in the coop. Consuela and Dolores were gone. In the yard, an old woman leaned on a cane.

Abuela? Her face was like a Taino arrowhead. Leathery wrinkles spread from her eyes. She pointed to the sky where shadows swam in the clouds like sharks.

I was a girl like you when they came. They took everyone. I went crazy. And hurt your mother. She thought you were like me. And you are. But you are special. You can stop them before the Awakening.

"Mom never knew." Maz bit her lip. The image of Dolores as a bitch was wrenched out, and in its place was a scared child. "How can I stop this?"

In there. This is where they take us.

Maz peered into the jungle. Sour wind crinkled her nose. She stomped into the jungle. Oily mud sucked her feet and splattered the hospital gown. Trees interlocked, and the last pencil-thin beams of moonlight vanished.

The forest was a living, angry thing. Twigs knotted around her ankles. Branches caught her wrists. Maz ripped free. She clambered up rocks. Terror was a compass. Wherever the forest fought, is where she dove in deepest. Her clothes were ripped to shreds.

Hungry eyes tracked her. Maz hurled a rock at them. And another. Her arms spun like medieval catapults. Forehead shined with sweat. She threw. Fingernails split. She threw. They scattered. She shouted the name of every one the vampires took Dolores. Consuela. And then she yelled her own name.

If they wanted to come for her, let them. She balanced a heavy rock from one hand to the other. Let them. She was too tired to be scared anymore. Fuck it. She kicked at watching eyes. And they left forever.

The jungle was afraid of Maz. She wrestled the trees. Foot on one. Hands on the other, she slid between branches as they lashed her cheeks and arms. Tumbling head first, she fell to the edge of a black lake. Obsidian ripples creased the surface. The trees and clouds moved in fast motion. She dipped a hand and pulled it out. Every finger was dry.

In the center of the lake was the First One. It was tall and bent like a crooked cell tower. Pairs of arms, moved spider-like in the gloom. Under its skin, hands and faces pressed as if dying to breathe. It buzzed with voices.

Maz kneeled and drank more shadows. The Coven's voices exploded between her temples. They whispered, cajoled, demanded, and pled across a web that spanned continents and centuries. Her skull felt like a broken, ceramic bowl.

Maz gulped more and her mind blew apart. Stars flew by. Planets whizzed by. Pink and red gassy clouds sparked new suns. The universe sped into her eyes, and it was noisy. Guttural yelps and mathematical music, warnings and pleas for help crisscrossed the void. The cosmos was boiling with life.

A giant, beehive-like ship sailed between solar systems. The vision aimed from inside it, out to the stars. Ethereal light and calm sound, filled the ship. Intricate, instant data pulsed like lightning in clouds of the collective mind. And then a hard slam. The ship plummeted to Earth. Terror was a strobe light. They crashed on Earth and tried to leave the wreckage, but air was poison. The atmosphere lay on them like a heavy rock.

The vision showed the silhouettes of a tribe on the hill. They crept close, spears out. The alien hive leapt on them. The scar-faced elder clutched his throat, and his lips shriveled. Two others tried to stand him upright. His skin dried into leather, and his eyes sank like rotten eggs. He burst to dust.

The humans fled to the cave and yelled at the others to run. Women hauled children on shoulders, but one by one, they burst into sparkling grains. A few fell and shook. Eyeballs turned obsidian. The hive entered flesh. The skin suffocated them. The ethereal telepathy narrowed into brain neurons. Breath tasted toxic. Pure energy could not live here, unless they stole these hairy, stinky bodies as hosts. They felt a desperate thirst.

The hive leapt from body to body. The further they left behind their original state, the foggier the memory of their true lives became, until only the oldest one among them could carry it. They thirsted for energy and hunted for it. The monkeys were easy to feed off. They ate their souls—the core spark of life, until dust caked their mouths.

The vision ricochet between aliens pretending to be human. One was a shaman. Another a priest. And then nobility and industrialists. Inching into the halls of power, they stoked hate and greed to cause chaos. Here one rode on horseback through the fields of wounded soldiers and bit the dying men to dust. Hunched over the bared neck, the vampire gored the man like a rag doll.

Maz almost vomited. The memories poured through her showing war, famine, genocide being orchestrated. They sailed ships filled with slaves from Africa and chewed into the bellies of men and women, until a pool of glittery sand lay next to the shackles. They licked the ovens at Auschwitz. And danced in the flames of Hiroshima, flickering into pure energy. The realization came. One nuclear war and they would be done with the thirst.

A blinding brightness, blasted the sky. Large, nuclear, mushroom clouds rose. Skeletons lifted hands in x-ray agony. After the heatwave, ash fell in hushed, grey drifts. The vampires emerged from the apocalypse like swimmers climbing out of the sea. Unsteady on land, they felt the ethereal light burn through their adopted flesh like wax. Slabs of skin, bone, nerves, and muscle fell. A humming brightness filled the space above their empty footprints. They rejoiced at their freedom and tossed the nuclear ash like Christmas snow.

Maz saw enough and stood up. She patted her body down to make sure it was all there, solid and breathing.

"So they want to kill us all," she said.

In the lake center was the First One, the oldest vampire, a twisted, fleshy tower that held them together. It radiated their whole history and their plan for the future.

She studied the dark currents that flowed by her hips. The trees on the shore that lashed out at her like angry mops. Rage spiked in her blood. The plan was clear. They wanted to kill us for centuries, and we gave them the means to do it. Nuclear war.

Maz waded to the shore and forced herself through trees. All this was another dimension. Time to get back. She focused on her hospital room. Under her feet, damp earth transformed into cool linoleum. The sickly, hospital smell filled her nose. Doors with shelved medical records appeared. One had her number. She saw herself sleeping in the bed. Maz sat next to Maz.

"Well, we've been through a lot." She touched the IV-tube spooling down to a needle in her arm. "We took pills. We numbed ourselves. We ran fast and far, right negra? Now we have to get out and end this war before it begins."

Maz removed the IV from the arm of her sleeping self.

"Time to wake up."

"What the hell is wrong with me?" Jesus asked

He downed aspirin to numb the headache. He moaned as the 'A' train rocketed through the tunnel. Batista rubbed his back.

They were going to Union Square. Batista bribed him to come to a Balk rally. He fanned himself with a spread of twenties and laughed an evil Hollywood villain laugh.

"Come to the Balk rally," he teased.

They stared and waited for who would break first. Jesus took the money.

"Come on," Jesus grumbled. "Let's go see Orange Hitler Jr."

They entire way there, Jesus rocked his head back and forth. In the park, he drained two water bottles.

"Bro, what's up?" Batista was scared.

Jesus sucked another bottle dry. He drank so hard that the plastic crinkled. Batista eyed him. Space had silently grown between them. Before they joshed and teased. Now Jesus was gone days at a time.

The whole neighborhood looked up to Jesus. Most guys blew fantasy lives into the air like smoke. Not Jesus. He had a map in his head. But now he was doing his Jesus-Saves-the-Hoes routine with this new girl Maz. Batista just wanted his brother back. Maybe at the Balk rally, they could play fight like the old days. He wanted Jesus to explain why he was wrong and he wanted to believe it.

At Union Square, the crowd filled the park. Banners that read, "Balk for President" blew back and forth. Red hats that read "Make America Great Again" looked like a thousand stop lights and in a way they were, saying "Stop" to all this change. Stop to the immigrants. Stop to the Muslims.

"They're here." Jesus manically pointed in every direction. "I can hear them."

"Bro, you're freaking me out." Batista gave him water. Jesus swigged it hard and threw the bottle.

"I'm hearing them and it's fucking splitting my wig."

Thundering applause shook the air as Balk walked on stage, arms spread, basking in the adulation. Jesus collapsed. Inside his brain, the sound of a high-piercing alarm, rattled every neuron. His brother lifted him back up.

Jesus felt the crowd was caught in some hypnotic pulse. It felt like a subliminal strobe light stroked them. He yanked out of his brother's arms. They wrestled and Jesus tore loose and jogged away.

Batista yelled, "What the hell is wrong with you?"

"Build that wall! Build that wall!" Balk was red-faced. Veins pulsed on his neck. He waved the red campaign hat like a flag to a bull. A hand reached up and turned the volume off. On the TV screen, Balk looked like an angry mime.

"Ms. Ramos," a nurse peered over her clipboard. Patients lounged on couches, zonked on drugs. Maz followed the nurse to a side room, where a woman in a casual suit sat across from an empty chair.

"Hello, I'm Ms. Flynn." She oozed professionalism.

Maz studied the therapist. Flynn shifted her weight. A strange, unreadable distance was in Maz's stare. It radiated peace, which was at odds with the schizophrenic, suicidal girl the records showed.

"How are you today?" she tilted her head.

"Much better," Maz smiled. "After finding out about my mom, I just couldn't anymore, but the drugs—Wow, they really, really helped. Thank you."

"How was your relationship with your mother?" Flynn pressed. The pain should be raw. The question should tug at the scab. But Maz smiled from a thousand lightyears away, on Planet Calm.

"She talks to me all the time," Maz said.

Flynn's eyes widened.

"Not like schizo voices." Maz slapped her knees. "No I dream about her. It's my way of healing our...you know...troubled relationship. I hear her in my dreams."

"Oh." Flynn's mouth eased. The pen hovered over the notepad.

"It's amazing the places you go in your dreams," Maz said. "All the people you meet."

AN INDIVIDUAL
IN A CROWD IS A
GRAIN OF SAND,
AMID OTHER
GRAINS OF
SAND THAT THE
WIND STIRS UP
AT WILL.

Eleven

SOMETHING'S WRONG.

Officer Butone studied the men in the cell. The fluorescent light, cast the bars of the jail onto them like a ruler, as if measuring their crime.

Something's wrong.

New York's jails were packed. And for the wrong kinds of crime. Not shootings. Not rapes. Not thefts. It was random, macabre violence. A teen knifed his grandmother into chunks and stuffed her in the closet, and fucked his girlfriend on the bed. The corpse fell out, and she screamed until the neighbors came. A wealthy, Upper East Side father put his baby in a blender. Kids in a playground tossed an autistic friend into traffic. He bounced off speeding cars like a beachball.

When Butone arrived on the scene, the perpetrators had dry, chapped lips and kept repeating the same word, "Thirst." It was scary. The whole precinct was on edge. No one knew what to do.

And then the city was eating itself alive with fear. A mob shouted outside the jail, calling for the death of the Muslim teens who burned their victims in that church. When the Muslims arrived, cops crowded the window to peek. Butone was shocked at how young they were, boys really, and zonked out.

Something's wrong.

Butone shuffled his paperwork like low-end poker cards. Curiosity got the best of him. He passed the interrogation room. Inside, Muslim kids trembled under lights. The looked gaunt, almost skeletal. The ambulance should have taken them to the hospital, but the Chief diverted it here. Chained to the desk, the ghoulish, stick-thin boys were given forms to sign.

"Did you kidnap these people?" Detectives jabbed at the paper in front of them. "Did you incinerate them? or contact Jihadist sites?"

In a catatonic haze, the Muslims signed their names. They were so shaky, detectives guided their hands as they wrote. Butone carried the image of half-starved boys helped by the police, to write their own confessions.

Something was wrong.

Butone went for coffee. In the hall, cops sat on plastic chairs and cheered the Balk rally. They raised fists as he thundered to let cops be cops, and stop tying their hands with bullshit, liberal laws. The news clip ended.

"Get ready for a bright night," the CNN newscaster said. "The Super Moon is here just in time for the presidential election. It will be the closest to Earth since 1948."

"The loonies are going to crawl out," Officer Roffstra said. He stretched the word looney like a rubber band.

"Overtime, man. Overtime," Officer Matiz—a tall, Dominican woman, threw imaginary dollar bills in the air, "Butone, you want to work the shift with us?"

"Loonies policing loonies," he said. "Let's save everyone the trouble and arrest ourselves."

Playfully, they gave him the middle finger. Butone laughed. Above him the TV showed the Super Moon with Balk's face.

"The Super Moon is here," the CNN newscaster said.

˅ ˅ ˅

Across the city, Maz stared at the moon on TV. Some producer at the station superimposed Balk's face on the moon. Dread trickled through her spine. The vampires were going to use Balk to ignite a nuclear war. He had to be killed.

"Maz Ramos," the nurse said. "You have a visitor."

Jesus poked his head in and shook flowers. They kissed and she tongued the pill they gave her into his mouth. He leaned over and fake coughed into the flowers. Maz knew the pill was lost in the beauty of roses.

They sat and held hands. Jesus saw the peaceful calm in her face. Her eyes didn't flutter. Her smile did not mask fear. It was a new Maz.

"I heard their plans," she kissed his forehead. "They want to kill us all."

"I can hear them Maz." Jesus nodded. "Loud and clear. Balk is with them. He's one of them. He's all in. Crazy. I went with my brother to the rally...long story...and when he got on stage, I got so thirsty, I drank everything..."

"How?" Maz squinted.

"Yo!" he pulled back. "I got it from you."

She tilted her head, leaned back, and her eyes popped wide.

"No. No. No." Her hands covered her crotch.

"Like Braveheart." he pretended to wipe her period blood off his face. "Freedom!"

"Stop it."

"Like Jim Jones' Kool Aid," He laughed. "You killing me."

"Stop it."

"I see dead people yo." He tapped his temple.

Maz leaned over and talked to her vagina. "See what you did to this nice man."

He snorted, slapped his knees.

"Can you teach me?" Jesus asked "How do hear them without going fucking crazy?"

His eyes were watery. Maz knew he was terrified but swallowed it to not break into a million, little pieces. She kissed his temples.

"Get me out of here," she whispered.

Are you ready to start the Awakening?

"Yes," Balk said. "Yes, I am."

We begin with a crash.

His cellphone vibrated and snapped him out of the trance. Balk read text after text of a crash on Wall Street. The Coven in finance orchestrated a global capitalist meltdown to set up his presidental campaign to save the day. All he had to do was play the role of the savior. Aides were knocking on the office door. He rose and let them in. They snapped and shouted like a pack of dogs.

"I know. I know." He marched out of the office, down to the lobby, and fired off orders to call a meeting. Outside, reporters snapped photos as he ducked into his limo. Melavia sat inside and fiddled with her rings.

He touched her. She moved away. The driver felt awkward in the quiet and drummed fingers on the steering wheel. The air was heavy.

No phone calls for a week. Melavia knew he had other women, but he called. With that call, she could hold her head up in public. Without it, she had to hide her shame with white coats and diamond necklaces. No phone calls for a week. Balk side-eyed her. She probably thought it was other women. What did it matter? After the Awakening, he would be immortal. He would live forever. And her. And his children. And his friends. And his business. Ashes.

The limo pulled to the college, Balk got out and looked at Melavia like a memory from another lifetime. He kissed her roughly and she pushed him back. He gripped her mouth, and smashed his lips on hers, and shoved her away.

Security men made a phalanx around him. Balk saw the auditorium and podiums where the presidential debate was being held. In less than an hour, Vice-President Shelly Canton would launch attacks at him on live TV. What about the free-falling economy? What about the sexual assault accusations?

Aides waved Apple Tablets. More news. More statistics. Balk giggled and chuckled. He turned his back on them, eyed the podiums.

"I think tonight," he said. "is going to be a good night."

∨ ∨ ∨

Angry men leaned over beers. More squeezed in. More hovered over their shoulders. Everyone in the bar stared at the TV. Balk strode to the podium, chest puffed out as he shook hands with Canton. He waved to the audience.

The men at the bar cheered. "Make America Great Again" hats were playfully pulled from heads and tossed like footballs. A bearded man waved a placard with a big super-moon and Balk's face on it. At the bar,

Balk moon pins shined on coats.

The PBS moderator began the debate. Balk and Canton knocked the questions back and forth like a ping-pong game. She was a hardened political vet. He was an off-the-cuff real estate mogul. They lobbed the latest headlines back and forth. What about the stock market crash? What about Muslim terrorism?

In the bar, they chanted "Lock her up! Lock her up!"

A trio of men drank rum shots and gave the finger to Canton.

"Don't know what she's saying half the goddamn time," one slurred

The man's stubbled face and expensive suit, spoke of late nights at the office. The twin brothers wore identical black jumpsuits and thin, gold chains.

"She's a fucking liar," they said.

Tongues licked lips like a pendulum. God, they were thirsty. No matter how much they drank, it was as if the beer vanished before hitting their guts. They ordered more. Dryness seeped into the lungs.

Outside a chant rose, low at first, then louder. The men turned.

"Stop fascism! STOP FACISM!"

Emptying the bar, Balk loyalists charged outside to see young college-aged protestors holding signs. The businessman tackled a young woman. The jumpsuit twins, elbowed activists to the sidewalk. A high-pitched scream split the air. The melee stopped. Everyone pointed at the business guy. The young woman's eyes dangled from his teeth.

"Thirst. Thirst. Thirst," he said.

Officer Butone arrived on the scene, horrified. The police lights spun and as red and white flashed on the faces the crowd seemed to close in.

"Get back." He waved his baton. "Get back."

On the sidewalk, a man sat with a blood-smeared mouth. He chewed out a young woman's eyes. He sat in a daze and licked his lips, constantly mumbling about thirst. Blood dotted his white shirt like an abstract painting.

Who does this? in broad daylight? It made him sick. The woman was on a gurney, yelling in pain as the ambulance doors closed. Butone tried to keep notes of who said what, but a sinking feeling hit him hard.

The scene in front of him was one in a series that no one connected. He'd seen this before. The perp with a dazed look and mumbling about thirst.

They lifted the handcuffed man into the cruiser. Butone shook his head. Morbid gawkers took cellphone videos.

"Get back." He waved at them. "Get back."

They sat on the bench and stared at the floor. Jail felt like a giant mouth closed on them. Breath or hope felt beyond reach.

"How long?" a slight brunette asked a tall, big-boned, blonde protester.

"Forever." She kicked the floor.

They swung their feet and waited. Time moved so slow, it became a weight.

"He ate her eye out," she whispered.

"I know." The tall blonde rubbed her face. "I keep seeing it." And tapped her temple.

"Tarp," she offered.

"Vicky."

They hugged intensely and squeezed wordless agony out. The screaming protester echoed endlessly in their minds.
"Tired," Tarp said.

"I know." Vicky stroked her hair.

The crowd banged the windows. Rage-twisted faces spread newspapers on the bank window that read, "WALL STREET CRASH!"

"Give me my damn money." A hardhat worker punched the window. It cracked.

The staff cowered behind desks. The glass door dripped with trash. A Latino family yanked on the door knob. They looked at their cellphones and craned necks to see Jesus across the street waving. Working through the crowd, they met.

"What's going on?" he asked.

"Trying to get our money." His dad scratched his beard. "They closed when news hit of the crash. Asshole pendejos."

Jesus sucked in his lips as they ranted about the crash. He didn't care. He just wanted to know if Maz could move in. But his parents couldn't hear him. They clenched and unclenched their fists. The mob punched the glass door and it shattered. They began to stampede in, when the hardhat yelled that Balk was on the news.

The mob snapped out of its hate. Heads bowed over phones. Balk's voice came out of dozens of small phone-speakers, as if he was chorus of men.

"The banks are in a freefall panic," he said. "I am calling heads of the major banks to an emergency meeting to stabilize our economy."

Relief eased their faces. A great wave had hung over them, its top curling as if it was about smash them to smithereens, but a giant hand pulled it back.

"America first," Balk said.

"America first! America first!" The mob cheered.

"I have to ask you something," Jesus pleaded.

"America first! America first!" His parents joined.

"I have to ask..." he said.

"America first," the newscaster said. "New York is cheering after

Ronald Balk announced a meeting with major bankers"

On the TV, New Yorkers waved red hats with the U.S. flag on them. The street was like a sea of boiling lava. Red everywhere. Maz's mouth was a flat, tight line. It was all wrong. All of it. Wrong.

"Some shadows walk on their own," a voice behind her said.

She turned and saw Sequan, the punk kid with a fro-hawk, tribal plugs in his ears, and a chestnut-brown face. His eyes twinkled with comical sagacity.

"They think we're crazy, right? Schizo? I never thought that. I never took their pills neither." He fluffed his fro-hawk. "Only reason to take them, is to get numb when the shadows get too loud."

He made the cuckoo sign with his finger circling his temple.

Maz got up.

"You ain't special," he said. "What you think? You goddamn Buffy the Vampire Slayer." He walked out of the room.

"Something big is about to happen," he said over his shoulder.

"Mom can she stay with us?" Jesus made a prayer sign with his hands. They had returned home. Water simmered on the stove.

"No," Batista said.

The family shot him a shut-the-hell-up look. And then Jesus threw him off his chair. The tablecloth on the dining table slid on the floor. Batista scrambled up and lunged at Jesus, but their father wrestled them apart.

"Enough!"

The brothers stared hard. The silence was a line of gunpowder. A violent spark sizzled across the silence.

"Why? Why does the schizo get to come here..." Batista trembled, "just because Romeo here is fucking her?"

Tears swayed on his face like earrings. He forearmed his eyes and left. He slammed the bedroom door shut and sat. How did a random girl get between them? The world was spinning crazy. And now Jesus caught religion over puta.

In the kitchen, the mother put the chair up.

"Do you love her?" she asked.

"I do," Jesus said.

"Well, try to love your brother too." She stacked plates and kissed his forehead. "He needs his big brother. Especially now. But go and get this Maz."

They embraced. He walked to his brother's room. Batista saw him and waved to leave him alone. Jesus sat next to him.

"Come with me to the hospital," he said. "Let's get her together."

In the strobe of camera flashes, dark-suited bankers marched into Balk Tower. The hall glinted with gaudy gold lining. Inside was quiet. The hard soles of business shoes echoed in the building.

They took the elevator up to Balk's office, where security guards stood like silent, armed sphinxes. One by one, Balk shook their hands. Each one anxiously judged who had power. The bald man from Bank of America wrote on a notepad, as the coiffed, Goldman Sachs woman whispered to a staffer. The room buzzed with calculations. Giant numbers hung above the nation. Numbers so large, they could crush millions of people.

Balk stirred his cup and saw his reflection in it. And then his face blossomed into many faces. The Coven stared from the dark cup. *You are one of us now.*

Balk felt his soul caressed by the voice of The First One.

You will live forever with us.

Balk looked around and saw executives from Bank of America, Goldman Sachs, and City Bank nodding behind sly poker faces.

We are here with you.

Balk heard two conversations; one very audible, but the other was telepathic. Like a ghostly whisper, underneath sound. On the wall, he saw the shadows of the executives caress, and lick, and bite each other as if a theater.

We are here with you.

They finished the deal and shook hands. Balk held open the door. The Bank of America executive waited at the doorway. His shadow crept on the carpet to the edge of sunlight, touched it and winced. It retreated back to the banker who touched Balk's shadow on the wall, gently like a lover, then left.

Maz thumbed books on vampires. Sunlight from the window brightened the illustrations. On the pages were foggy castles, white ghouls with long fingernails, nobles drooling over the bared neck of a peasant girl, or a shadow creeping up the walls. Vampires, no matter what age or what continent, suffered from thirst.

The same story wove the books together. Here it was myth. Here it was a romantic novel. Here it was a Hollywood film or a TV series. Here it was Karl Marx's *Capital* or *The Communist Manifesto*, where a ruling class was portrayed as vampires living off the workers. Maz saw herself as a minor character in this story and now, her role would come its last chapter.

She packed her toothbrush, books, and clothes in her backpack. In a few hours, Jesus was on his way. His family said to bring her home. It was a sweet gesture, if meaningless. Sure they would invite her to dinner, maybe pass knowing looks thinking this is their new step-daughter. But the world would end soon.

Maz picked up her cell phone and read the news about the Super Moon. Millions of people were going to vote. She already knew Balk would win. The vampires would use him to start a nuclear war. It was her job to kill him.

Maz didn't tell Jesus. Sometimes, she daydreamed of them playing with their child's toes. She sighed and put another book in her backpack. Sequan appeared at the door in regular street-clothes.

"How many more are there?" Maz asked. "Like us. Who can hear them? is it just you? Tell me it's not just you."

"There's others." he carefully stepped into her room like a man making his way across a minefield. "A lot have been killed by them. A lot killed themselves. Couldn't cope with the noise or the knowing what it was, you know, the whole network of vampires that ruled our world. It's kind of heavy knowledge."

She patted the bed next to her. He sat down, flipped through her books.

"Capital? The Communist Manifesto?"

"Capital is dead labor, which vampire-like..." Maz intoned in a wistful monotone. "It lives only by sucking living labor and lives the more, the more labor it sucks." She took the book from Sequan. "They've been with us for a long time. We live in their world."

They studied each other. She searched his face for emotional scars. Was he suicidal? Was he deluded by visions of martyrdom? Was he broken?

He wondered how much she knew. How far could she hear them? How close did she get to their plans? Did she know what all the noise meant?

"Where are the others?" Maz asked.

"Right now. It's just me." He shrugged.

Her mouth made a large 'O'. She giggled, hiccupped and laughed.

"It's just me," she imitated. "It's just me." Falling back on the bed, she cackled so hard she farted, which made her roar even more.

Caught by surprise, Sequan smiled. "Just me."

"Just you." Maz walked to the window. The moon hung in the day like a lost cue ball from a pool table. She wiped away laugh-tears.

"Well, okay then. We are officially fucked." Her mouth twisted in disgust. "The rebel fleet is not coming to Endor. No sir." Grabbing her backpack, she reached for her coat. Fuck waiting for Jesus. She didn't have time for him or this hospital. The nurse gave her discharge papers.

"Hey wait, wait," Sequan raised his voice. "I came to recruit you, build a cell, and start to organize. This is larger than any one of us trying to go all solo."

"Do you have any idea how big this is?" Maz locked eyes with him and step by step, walked slowly to him, "do you?"

Sequan flinched. How dare she? Did she know what it was like being called a freak? Did she know how he hid inside of closets? Or how hearing the vampires shattered his mind like glass and how it took months to pick up the pieces?

Maz bit her lip until blood sopped out and kissed him. Sequan struggled, but she gripped him like a vice. Mouth on mouth they fought and skidded across the room. Sneakers squeaked on the linoleum. A powerful pulse blasted his brain. He saw nuclear mushroom clouds.

"Now you will see how big it is." She kissed him deeper.

Twelve

DRUG DEAL?

Officer Butone tracked two men into an alley. The dealer was a stocky guy, with an Al Pacino, Serpico beard and shabby FUBU clothes. A small plastic-bag turned in his palm. The buyer was a tall Black guy sporting a godawful 90's goatee. Shooting furtive glances up and down the street, they ducked in.

Butone was in plain clothes. Dirt crunched underfoot. Call backup. Call back. The buzz of adrenaline was a steam-train. Hand on his gun, he edged in.

Shadows were thick, black curtains. Butone aimed his flashlight, thumbed it on. The bright illumination, showed the dealer chomping off the customer's arm. Sparkly dust blew around his mouth. Another bite. The buyer's head rolled onto the pavement. Butone dropped the flashlight, drew his gun, and fired.

Each muzzle flash was a photograph. The naked man gripped the head like a football. Another gunshot. He climbed a wall. Another gunshot. The alley was empty.

"Please. Please. Please. Please." Butone scrambled for his flashlight, found it and turned it back on. Drizzle speckled the beam. The FUBU clothes were in a pile. He got up. His temples throbbed. He gripped his gun like a blind man's cane. .

He picked up the clothes. Glittery dust fell out of the pants.
What? Who?

"I just want to pop it." Vicky pretended to pinch the plump moon. A pale glow fell on New York like ephemeral snow.

"I think your arm needs to be a bit longer," Tarp said.

They both jumped at the moon.

"Isn't the meeting started? Come on." Vicky tugged Tarp into the maze of Liberty City. Silhouettes moved between tents. Activists traded clothes or recharged cellphones. The camp grew on the Great Lawn of Central Park. It was surrounded by police and combed through by reporters for tales of road-roughened Leftists.

The air hummed with hope and fear. They painted signs and wore flowers to declare that it was a non-violent protest, but they were scared. New Yorkers cursed and bumped them from the side walk. Some spat on them. It was Balk, damn Balk. He had hypnotized every-one from the TV screens. He first looked like a clown with his odd, orange comb-over glistening like a helmet, but that easy contempt felt like a thousand years ago, when they could take for granted the world was sane.

Each day his grip on the city grew. Last night, Balk waved copies of the NY Post at a rally with the headline that Muslim teens confessed to incinerating victims. Look! Criminal immigrants! Terrorists! New Yorkers listened. And why wouldn't they. The Wall Street crash threw the city into a bottomless shadow. Riots convulsed the streets until Balk, damn Balk, called a meeting and pulled the nation back from disaster.

No one was feeling protesters now. Young men wore Balk's face on their shirts and patrolled the city. When activists demonstrated, the Balk militia tore the signs from their hands. Or worse.

Tarp and Vicky saw panic in everyone's eyes. Liberty City which began as a beautiful carnival of love, a protest against Balk, was now seen as threatening the one man who rescued America. And now police surrounded the camp. Helmets and batons glistened in the moonlight.

"Look at them." Vicky pursed her lips. "They cannot wait to deliver the beat down of all beat downs."

"Tarp?"

She turned around. Tarp hugged a young, black man, sporting a fro-hawk and a hospital band on his wrist. Next to him was a brown, Latina teen with impatient eyes.

"The meeting," Vicky said.

Tarp tried to hug the Latina, but she did not hug back. She stood like a statue. The young man felt the energy change and tried to smile.

"I'm Sequan." He held out his hand. Vicky shook it. Awkward.

"Here's my friend Maz," he said.

"I need a gun," Maz said. "I need a gun because I am going to kill Ronald Balk."

∨ ∨ ∨

"Maz? where are you?" Jesus peeked into room after room. Batista felt sadness and anger slosh in his stomach. Bitch wasn't here.

"She left," the nurse said, "hours ago."

He stiffened and asked the nurse where. She didn't know. Batista focused on his shoes, he didn't want to see his brother's eyes water. Why is he tripping so hard on this girl? Why couldn't she wait?

"Bro, let's go. She ain't worth it man, let's go."

Jesus had already dialed her number.

"Bro, come on." He tugged Jesus who shook him off and ran down the hall. Batista sprinted after him and wedged into the elevator. The brothers circled each other.

"Where are you going?"

"I don't know," Jesus said. "I don't know.

∨ ∨ ∨

Butone filed the report. Just another shooting in a city. Older cops said he was baptized. They said the gun's kickback throbs in the mind long after it's holstered. They said he would deal with the questions for days. Did I do the right thing? What if I had been killed? What if I had killed?

He was one of them now. Butone smiled weakly, shrinking from the brotherly slaps on his shoulder. The one thing he needed to say, was swallowed down. He didn't shoot at a person. Whatever it was. It wasn't human.

He walked into the meeting room. The Chief of Police strode back and forth. Deep age lines creased his face. A ring of officers sat at the table. Butone sat down. He waved. Why were they here? Two were women—dark-haired, one Black, one Latina. The Chief placed folders in front of them. Operation Liberty it read.

"We need baby faces." He hiked up his belt to belly-level. "Militants are planning attacks, and we want to grab them before the white shirts bulldoze the protest."

Butone read the mission outline. Some photos were mugshots, some were hazy photos taken by surveillance teams, and others were Facebook pictures. Young, tattooed, and tattered they had the "The Look", a wild, expression as if entranced by a light.

"You will contact your targets," the Chief said. "Get intel and set up a sting operation. Weapons. Conspiracy."

Butone licked his chapped lips. He was so thirsty. The other cops tongued lips too. He glanced at their folders, bits of dry skin dusted them like bread crumbs.

ⱽ ⱽ ⱽ

Jesus dialed Maz over and over. Someone knocked on the door of his room.

"Not now," he shouted.

"Open up," Batista pleaded.

Jesus bent over his phone. Lightning struck his brain. Pain. Pain. Lips flaked and mouth became arid. Batista pounded the door. Jesus fell on the floor, grabbed a pillow and folded it around his head. Voices pounded him.

Thirst. Thirst. Thirst.

He got on his knees. Legs wobbled like toothpicks. At the window, he saw Butt, Sam and Trey, the local "Safety Militia". They talked to Trey's uncle, Charlemagne.

Jesus never liked him. He was too old to be running the streets. A semi-retired gangster from the old days, who strutted like a ghetto peacock. He polished gold on the stoop, bragged that he fucked this nigga up, or shot that nigga, or lay the pipe on that bitch and can't tell me nothing about nothing. Jesus hated his ass.

Jesus shook his head and breathed. Focus. Focus. Charlemagne's shadow was cast on the wall behind him and moved on its own. It actually sniffed at the boys like a dog. They didn't see it but he did.

"I got you." Jesus pointed at Charlemagne. Batista pounded the door. Jesus opened it. His brother stood, mouth a tight line.

"What's going on?"

Jesus hugged him. Batista was shocked. Hermano was not the touchy-feely type. Now they held each other like toddlers.

"Baby brother." Jesus held Batista's face in his hands. "I love you. I want you to do me a favor. Stay away from the Balk rallies. You want to vote for the guy, go ahead, fucking vote, but stay away from them."

"What's wrong with you?"

But Jesus ran out into the street and hollered to Charlemagne.

ᵥ ᵥ ᵥ

"A gun," Tarp squeaked.

"A gun," Maz said flatly.

Glances boomeranged from face to face.

"You want a Gatling gun or would a regular Uzi do?" Vicky snapped.

Maz smiled.

"It's not funny." Vicky pointed a sharp finger. Tarp grabbed at her sleeve. "No. Get off me. It's not funny. This is a protest camp. Cops are horny to beat the living daylights out of us and we're being peaceful. They catch wind that some street urchin who saw the Matrix too many times, is trying to get her hands on a fucking gun and we're going to get our skulls bashed in. DO YOU GET IT?"

"Vicky," Tarp whispered.

"No. No don't Vicky me. This is the kind of bullshit that gets people killed or thrown in jail for their whole lives. I want you out." She aimed her forefinger at Maz. "Out of the camp."

Maz cocked her thumb like a gun, her forefinger a barrel aimed at Vicky.

"I know something that you don't." Maz swung her gun-hand at Tarp. "Neither do you." Then aimed at Sequan. "But you know. We don't have a lot of time left. Tell them brother-man."

Vicky and Tarp asked him with their eyes *What-Drug-Is-She-On?* A grim light smoldered in his eyes.

"We intercepted messages from a secret society that is using Balk to start a war," he said. "If he gets elected, all of this..." He made big circles with his hands and mimed a big explosion.

"We can show you the messages," Maz said in dry monotone. "You think we're crazy. Who wouldn't think that but I'll show you proof."

Tarp trembled. Vicky stared at Maz with a sad, pitying expression like a grandmother with a dull child.

"Come on," Vicky countered. "What are you going to show us, some website? Is that your proof, a website? Maybe it will say who killed JFK?"

Maz nodded at Sequan. "Let's not waste time."

He unzipped the tent, ushered them in. They sat down in a circle, and he pulled out a knife from his backpack.

ᐯ ᐳ ᐯ

"I see you." Jesus crept behind Charlemagne and Trey.

The closer he got, the dryer his mouth got. It was a radar to track them as they slipped into a hollowed out building. Charlemagne pushed the front door off its hinges. Trey squirmed in. The street was like a deserted war zone. Glass shards on the sidewalk. Trash swept up into small tornados by the breeze.

Jesus climbed through a broken window. He gingerly set himself down. It was dark and cool inside the brownstone.

"Please stop!" Trey yelled.

The scream came from the second floor. Jesus grabbed a rock and sprinted up the stairs. He lunged into a room. Half of Trey was on the floor. He blinked and asked where his legs were. Glittering dust pooled around him. Jesus scooped the dust back into the pant legs while Trey asked where his feet were.

The boy's jaw fell. The top half of the skull collapsed. He was gone. Jesus kneeled in a thin film of glitter and wept.

He's dead. He's dead. He's dead. Jesus ferociously wiped the dust off. A shadow moved in the hall. Charlemagne was there.

⌄ ⌄ ⌄

"Did you ever read *Plato's Allegory of the Cave*?" Maz licked Sequan's knife until her tongue bled. "Did you know the man in chains doesn't leave the cave? No, my dears, he is forced out."

Vicky and Tarp turned and fumbled the tent zipper. Maz and Sequan slipped cold blades under their chins.

"I am forcing you out of the cave tonight." She kissed Vicky. Sequan kissed Tarp then pulled back. His mouth was bloody.

The women vomited a gooey sticky stream. A strobe light hit their neurons like a hammer hits an anvil. They clutched their heads. Mouths dried up. Stomachs knotted. They moaned on the tent floor.

"Strong juice you got there." Sequan wrapped Tarp's hands in duct tape.

"Strong enough." Maz taped Vicky's wrists.

They unzipped the tent and stepped out into the clear night. Protesters waved as they passed. The tents next to them were empty. Everyone was at the council meeting.

"How long?" Sequan handed Maz a flask of rum.

"Few hours." She swigged it.

"How long will it take them to be useful?" he asked. "Took me years. And we have until the Super Moon."

Tarp and Vicky vomited again. Maz and Sequan waited to see if the girls were going to get louder but nothing. They shrugged.

"Did you really read Plato's Allegory of the Cave," he teased.

"Of course I did." She play-pushed him. "Just because I went to public school, doesn't mean I'm illiterate."

"Do you think Plato knew about them?" He stared at the moon.

"He knew." She studied the moon too. It was a bright, pale stopwatch ticking to the End Times. Maz took out her cellphone and dialed Jesus.

"Where are you?" crooned Charlemagne. "I'm thirsty." A low giggle echoed through the halls.

Jesus gripped the door frame, peered into the dark. The house was covered in hues of midnight. The creeping sound of Charlemagne was a song of terror.

"I'm thirsty,"

Jesus phone rang. Maz's face was the caller ID. Fuck. Frantically he cupped hands over it. The cellphone light cast a shadow on the wall. It had long dagger like fingers. Jesus grabbed the rock and hurled it, but the sweat on his palms sent it awry. It hit the shadow. Charlemagne yelled in pain.

What? He picked up the rock and hit the shadow again. Charlemagne moaned. Jesus brought the rock down on the shadow. It lifted its hands like a gothic painting. And from the next room stumbled Charlemagne. Blood spurted from his mouth. Each time Jesus hit the shadow, more teeth flew from the vampire's mouth. Blood oozed like smeared roses. Jesus stopped. His phone rang again. It was Maz.

Is he going to pick up or not? Lord knows, he texted her all the time. Once Maz stuffed it in her underwear and let it tingle like a dildo because he texted her for half an hour straight. Now he was AWOL?

Whooping came from the Council meeting. A leathery-faced woman with cornrows guided them like a ringmaster. Stragglers walked with signs on shoulders like hobos. A NYPD helicopter probed Liberty City with a searchlight that looked like a giant, white finger.

"Maz?"

"Jesus?"

"I got one," he panted. "I got one. Right here. It's alive. Right, you undead bitch?"

Maz heard Jesus kicking someone.

"You got one?" she made a face at Sequan. "You mean a vampire?"

"Yes! What do I do with it?"

"Run away!" She imagined Jesus going poof in a cloud of dust.

"How do you kill it?" he asked.

"How do you kill it? I don't know how to kill them. What do I look like? a vampire whisperer?"

"Don't you study up on this?" He barked. "Aren't you the Queen of the Vampires? Can't you hear them yapping all the time? Figure it out!"

He hung up. Maz was flabbergasted. She told Sequan that Jesus caught a vampire. He stared blankly, as if not understanding her. She said it again, slowly. He rubbed palms on his face.

"This is a lot," Sequan said. "This is a lot."

Maz dipped into the tent. Tarp and Vicky rolled around, eyes closed, and breathing in short bursts. Yep, they hit peak of awareness. Time and space were being ripped apart. Hearing all the vampires for the first time is terrifying.

"Excuse me." Maz crawled over them to her backpack to pull out books. She put her feet on Tarp and Vicky as they convulsed, and casually skimmed the pages. So what kills vampires? Some ideas were dumb. stakes through the heart? No. decapitation? Interesting. garlic? The only thing that kills, is breath.

"Hey," She nudged the girls. "You know how to kill a vampire?"

They blindly pawed the air.

"No of course you don't," Maz sighed.

Sequan squeezed into the tent and thumbed open the eyes of Vicky and Tarp like a doctor.

"They're peaking," he said. "When they come down, we need to teach them how to focus. Bringing them to the light is cool, but what's the point if they pop?"

Maz closed her book.

"Sir, yes sir!" she stuffed her backpack. "Let me go to Jesus and figure this out. If we can find out what kills them, then it will help us when we try to take out Balk. Can you take care of our students?"

He twisted open a water bottle, tilted Tarp's head up, and poured some into her mouth. "Thirst," she mumbled.

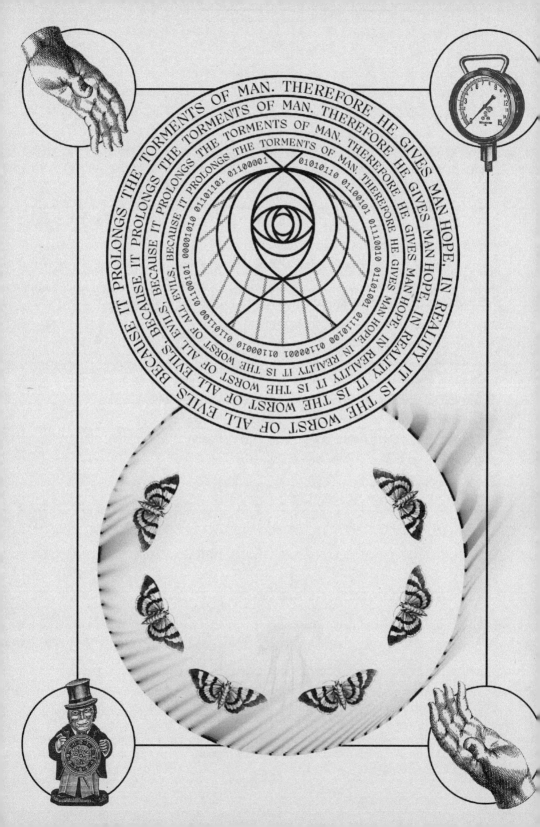

THE TORMENTS OF MAN. THEREFORE HE GIVES MAN HOPE, IN REALITY IT IS THE WORST OF ALL EVILS. BECAUSE IT PROLONGS THE TORMENTS OF MAN. THEREFORE HE GIVES MAN HOPE, IN REALITY IT IS THE WORST OF ALL EVILS. BECAUSE IT PROLONGS THE TORMENTS OF MAN. THEREFORE HE GIVES MAN HOPE, IN REALITY IT IS THE WORST OF ALL EVILS. BECAUSE IT PROLONGS

01010110 01100101 01110010 01101001 01110100 01100001 01110011
00001010 01101101 01100001 01101100 01101100

Thirteen

"WHOSE STREETS? OUR STREETS!"

Butone held a sign of a pig dressed as a banker. The march passed a row of banks. Some had cracked windows. Some had paint splattered on them like giant birdshit. New Yorkers eyed them suspiciously.

A red-haired woman next to him wearing a Palestinian scarf, offered him water. Next to him, a gay man with a pink triangle on his shirt, gave him a pamphlet. They looked at him with easy friendship. No suspicion.

They didn't see his cop life. They saw a Black man wearing anti-war, anti-Balk, anti-racism pins. For all they knew, he was the most down-ass Lefty out here.

"This is great," he talk-shouted to them. "I don't want this to ever end."

"It won't," she said. "The movement is forever."

"I just feel like we need more than marching right now," Butone recited the script. "Balk is really unhinged, crazy. All this marching isn't going to stop him."

The march turned a corner. They shook the air with chants as police on motorcycles followed. Cops held rolls of orange, plastic netting. At some point, the order would come down, and they'd secure the street and haul protesters in like squirming fish.

The plan? Get arrested. In the cell, say he's going to kill Balk and knew a guy with guns. Lay it out. Entice them. Say Balk is too dangerous for liberal strategies. It's time to take him down.

For now, he marched and a cop on the sidewalk, blew him a kiss. Jokers. They love this spy and dagger stuff.

"What do you think should be done?" the pink-triangle man asked.

"I don't know," Butone answered. "Something more than this. Is his one life worth everyone's? Do we just let it happen because of liberal piety ...cause he's the goddamn president?"

Three activists in front said they felt the same. Butone hefted the sign higher.

"Where are you?" Maz whispered.

The gutted building had cobwebs billowing in the corners. She side-stepped broken glass. It brought back memories of life as a runaway. How many ruined apartments had she slept in? How much fear of crews of horny boys hunting for someone to beat up or rape? She hated that life so much.

"Up here," Jesus said.

Maz trotted up the stairs. Her heart was a jackhammer. He got one? he really got one? She followed his voice into a room. Jesus held a cellphone above a middle-aged man, tied to a chair. The man's head was bloody. Teeth were missing.

"This is it?" she hissed.

"You want me to bring him to you in a fucking coffin?" Jesus snarled.

"Dressed in a tux and speaking Transylvanian?"

He kicked Charlemagne's leg. Maz stopped him.

"I saw homeboy here kill his own nephew." Jesus circled him. "But I got the drop on him. Lucky me or I would've been swept up with a broom and thrown into the trash. No, he's trying to play human, but I got you homeboy, I got you."

Jesus pointed at the man's shadow on the wall. Charlemagne sat still, but it lashed out as if trying to unknot itself from the body in pain.

Picking up a rock from the floor, Jesus wiggled it in front of Maz then knocked the shadow on the jaw. Charlemagne's mouth was wrenched out of place. He began to cry.

"See," Jesus said.

"Holy shit." Maz clapped him on the back. She unzipped her backpack, took out garlic, a Christian cross, a super-soaker water gun, a stake, and a long kitchen knife.

"Oh nice." Jesus fingered the tools. "This is like an episode of "24"."

"You know I was thinking the same thing." She smeared the garlic on Charlemagne's face. They waited. Nothing. He blinked with swollen eyes and sniffed himself. Now he stank too.

"Hmm, what about this?" Maz picked up the super-soaker and cocked it.

"Holy water?"

"From a real church." She doused Charlemagne. Smoke rose from burning skin. He rocked in torment. They laughed as Jesus gagged him with a sock.

"Well that's useful to know," she said. "Let's try the cross."

"It's gonna be okay." Sequan cupped Tarp's head in his hands.

"Make them stop," she begged.

"I... I... I don't want this." Vicky fumbled to unzip the tent.

Sequan pushed her gently back down. He wouldn't blame her if she hated him forever. No one would want this. No one could live a normal after knowing the truth.

Tarp sat up.

"I thought you dosed us with LSD." Her hands trembled like a bird. Sequan held them. "Thirst. I felt their thirst. It wasn't LSD. And Balk..."

Sequan let her hands go. "Balk is with them."

"Can they hear us?" Rage, fear and wonder churned in her face.

"No. Not yet anyway.' He checked his cellphone. Max had texted him. He threw on his jacket and helped Tarp out of the tent. The tents of Liberty City glowed under the Super Moon.

"What can we do?" she asked.

"We have to stop them," he said. "Before they start a nuclear war."

Tarp sniffed the dried vomit on her shirt, turned to the tent to get wet naps, and shrieked. Sequan looked. It was empty. Vicky was gone.

Thirst. Thirst. Thirst.

Vicky lurched foot to foot. She pressed palms on the sides of her head to squeeze the voices out.

"Please. Please. Please stop."

She stumbled on the side paths of Central Park, found a water fountain and splashed her cheeks. Acidic rage boiled. They dosed her.

Thirst. Thirst. Thirst.

"I don't want this," she said. "I don't want this."

She heard voices. They laughed, and it scraped the inside of her skull like razors. Did the drug destroy her brain? would she hear strange voices forever? Goddamn that Latina bitch.

"Vicky," someone shouted. "Vicky, Hey Vicky."

Kate, a long-time friend waved to her. Ben too. The pink triangle on his shirt like a badge. Next to him was Butone in a denim jacket. They instantly knew. A million judgements scrolled behind their eyes.

"I WAS DOSED," Vicky screamed. "I WAS DOSED!"

They cradled her as she sobbed. Vicky told them about Maz and her crazy vampire theory. Ben said he'd get help. Kate wanted to get legal help, but neither wanted to leave Vicky alone.

"I'll stay with her," Butone said. "I had folks who had bad trips. I'll stay with her." He shooed them. "Go." They asked Vicky with their eyes. She nodded. Promising to come back, they ran to Liberty City. He sat next to her, pulled out a packed of powdered vitamin, poured it into his water bottle, and shook it.

Vicky gulped it down. Burped.

"Vampires?" he asked.

"Vampires." She chuckled bitterly.

"Just in case." He lit a cigarette and gave it to her. "You don't have enough chemicals in your body."

"Thanks." Vicky coughed. "I don't even know you but thanks. You know the point is to trust. Build a new world. And this cunt doses me."

"Vampires?" he asked again.

"Maz is her name. She tongued acid into me. Talked about vampires who drain people to dust, travel between shadows and come from space. Said Balk was one of them. I was tripping so hard, I thought it was true. Can you believe that?"

Vicky saw his hands shake. Her cellphone buzzed. She read the text message and almost dropped it.

"They caught one," she said. "They caught a vampire."

She held the screen to him. On it battered middle aged man plead-ed for his life. Maz leaned over, and gave the peace sign. Jesus dry humped his head.

"I think they might be killing a man," Vicky said. "They're insane."

∨ ∨ ∨

"They're here," Maz see-saw waved at Sequan and Tarp who anxiously stood in front of the building. She ran downstairs, swung open the door, and hugged them. Tarp did not hug back. That's fair she thought.

"Where's Vicky." Maz glanced down the street.

"She left." Sequan studied his shoes.

"She left?" Maz exploded. "She left?"

"I almost left," Tarp jutted a finger into Maz's chest. "It's too much."

"Boo hoo." Maz mimicked a baby crying. "Come in. We have some-thing to show you." She motioned them inside. They went up the stairs, when someone knocked on the door. Maz gave a hand signal to wait. Near the window, she peaked at the stoop. Vicky stood there with a tall, bald Black man. Maz's chest kicked in fear. Who was he?

She grabbed the knife and stood against the door. They came in. She tackled the new guy. The knife point was at his neck.

"Shhhhh." Maz put a finger to her lips.

Vicky lunged at her, but Jesus pinned her arms. Butone saw the knife in close up. Everyone's reflections were stretched on the blade like spirits caught between worlds. A sick, feverish glow radiated from Maz. He knew she could kill him.

"I saw one too," he stammered.

Maz shifted on top of him, glanced at Vicky, then Tarp. Sequan rubbed his hands, as if going to Thanksgiving dinner.

"You two can frolic all you want." he jogged upstairs. "I came to see a vampire."

Tarp followed him. Jesus said to go to the roof. Vicky sat up, blew a hair from her face and joined them. Maz kissed Butone. He squirmed but the knifepoint dug into his neck.

"Now you're family," she said. "I'll see you on the roof."

Maz ran up the stairs. Butone sprang to his feet and saw blood on his sleeve like red crayon. Cursing them, he climbed the ladder to the roof. The early morning air tingled on his neck.

They stood in a half circle. Maz, Vicky, Tarp and the young brother with the fro-hawk. A battered hoodrat was tied to a chair. His eyes were swollen and his jaw was bent like a broken doll. Maz and Jesus tossed garlic back and forth. Vicky and Tarp stood, eyes wide like snowballs. Butone felt dizzy. Dryness wracked his mouth.

"Well the gang is all here." Maz spread her arms. She was dressed in all black like a magician. The sky was dark turquoise. Everyone looked like smudged charcoal drawings, half in and half out of the twilight.

"Get down on the ground." Butone pulled out a badge and gun. No one looked at him. Charlemagne thrashed in the seat. The sun opened like a fan across the sky. Birds chirped. In the street, a city garbage truck rattled by, parting the quiet, it passed and the silence folded over them.

Flames ignited on skin. Charlemagne snapped at them like a snake. Under his face was a monstrous alien. Large insect like eyes. Rows of needle teeth. Fire swirled around him. And he burst into ash. Empty clothes fell on the seat. His sneakers smoldered. Butone dropped his gun and badge. Maz scooped the ash and motioned for everyone to come. They did and one by one, she thumbed ash on their tongues.

"In the name of the Father, the Son and the Holy Ghost." She kissed them.

Butone convulsed in shock and fear. They were real. Whatever they were, they weren't human and they were real. Maz held a pinch of ash between her fingers. He opened his mouth wide and received her blessing.

"Amen," he said. "Amen."

I AM HERE
ALONE
AT THE END
OF THE
WORLD.
I REACH
OUT
AND TOUCH
NOTHING.

Fourteen

"I AM IMMORTAL."

Balk lifted from the roof. The moon light tasted delicious. Up. Up. Up. New York looked like an anthill. "I am forever."

He lowered himself to the roof. Construction tools and tarp, flapped around naked steel girders that jutted like a metal ribcage. He scooped up his clothes and descended to the office. Everyone was in bed. He didn't need to sleep anymore. Or eat. Or even be human. The old Balk was a tiny, weak shell. It had burst apart.

He sat on the chair and heard the Coven. They were thirsty. They needed the First One. They buzzed eagerly for the Awakening.

Thirst. Thirst. Thirst.

Shadows spilled into his office like puddles of ink. The last one slipped by his feet as between the buildings, the sun throbbed yellow. It hurt his skin like a low microwave. And then a man's face appeared in his mind. He was tied to a chair, catching fire and dying. Searing pain shot out like electricity through the telepathic link and stopped.

Balk held throat. One of them had died. But how?

∨ ∨ ∨

"We gotta kill him." Maz measured their commitment. Can they kill? Can they die? All five lay sprawled like dolls with their strings cut. They stared at the sky. Clouds billowed across New York as dark, heavy mountains of mist.

She asked them to close their eyes. They did.

Can you hear me?

Each blinked rapidly. Maz was a faraway radio in their heads

Yes I can hear you. Me too. I can. We all hear you. How did this happen? Can they hear us? What does this mean?

Maz stood up. Stepped between them.

Listen. All of you listen.

They interlaced arms and formed a kind of human igloo, curved inward so their heads touched. Hot breath steamed their faces.

He is almost one of them. If he wins, he'll start a nuclear war. Then they take over. We have to kill him.

But how? What happens to us?

It doesn't matter what happens to us. It just doesn't.

Tarp wept. Vicky nodded stoically. Butone blew long, corrugated breaths. Jesus and Sequan had their arms around Maz, as if in a silent tug of war. She felt their possessiveness but focused on her own memories. Her life appeared in their minds. They saw a child taking pills and the Lake of Shadows, where the First One stood between worlds and commanded the Coven.

Tarp tried to wiggle out of the memories. Maz gripped her even tighter.

Follow me.

They saw the Coven stretched like a phosphorous web around the world. At the bottom, crawled psychopaths, pimps and sex traffickers. At the peak, presidents, bankers and generals at polished desks. All of them killed, relentlessly killed. The First One was at the center, a bright murderous star, sending and receiving their thirst.

They saw a man at the window of the White House. On the glass was the reflection of a nuclear mushroom cloud. God-sized pain broke the huddle. Each one vomited and screamed. Maz stood and watched them writhe in spasms. She reached up, as if catching the nuclear ash that fell like snow.

˅ ˅ ˅

"In just three days the election will take place." The reporter held the microphone to the young man. "What do you hope will happen?"

He smirked a sinister half-smile.

"Balk's gonna win. He's gonna win big. Feel me? Big." He jutted a forefinger into the camera. "He saved our city and America and he ain't even president yet."

"What about the critics who say Balk has split Latinos, pitting older, established groups like Puerto Ricans and Dominicans against Mexicans?" the reporter asked. "Calling Mexicans rapists and illegals?"

The young man stared back at the camera, eyes glassy with joyful rage.

"American jobs are for Americans. We got enough problems without them." He blew a kiss. "That means you Speedy Gonzalez!"

Batista shoved the reporter back and rejoined the march. Thousands shook the streets with chants of "America First". Batista felt bones rattle and a buzz in the skull from the vibration. Dizzy, hot and angry, he followed the march. Balk was a hero. Balk let them be strong again.

Batista saw anti-Balk protesters on the sidewalk. They waved signs too. The street looked like a poker table with giant cards. He ran over and tore a Balk mask off the head of an activist and stomped it. He felt like it wasn't just an election but a gamble for his very life. If Balk won, we'd have a chance to recreate America. And Batista wanted to be reborn.

The years ahead were one dull, endless job. His family were workers and that's it. He saw it. But not Jesus. He was chasing the schizo, puta Maz. He hated her deeply.

Maybe he'd run into her at Liberty City? After the rally, he was told that everyone was going to kick them out of New York. The sinister half-smile reappeared on his face. The march turned a corner.

∨ ∨ ∨

"Look at it." Tarp pointed at the Super Moon. It hung in the sky like a polished clock. They sat on the rooftop, faces puffy and tear streaked.

"The Super Moon." Vicky looked up. "How can we stop the End Times?"

Butone, Jesus, Sequan and Maz traded glances. She pursed her lips. Jesus cracked his knuckles.

"Suicide bomb? or just straight stab him?" Sequan asked.

"Bro, when did you join ISIS?" Jesus teased. He pantomimed pulling a string on a vest and blowing up.

Maz shook her head.

"It's not him. It's the First One," she said. "We have to get to Balk Tower and kill it. If we don't, then there'll be another Balk and then another one."

"I can get a detail at the Tower," Butone said. "It's got round the clock NYPD and Secret Service protection. I can get us in."

They nodded. Jesus said whatever they decided, he was cool with it. He left to go pee. They watched him go downstairs.

"Ok," Maz said. "How will you get us in? The place is packed with security. We don't have a layout of the building. We just know he's in there somewhere."

"I don't know." Butone upturned his hands. "I don't know."

"Guess we're going to have to clean up," she rolled her eyes. "Ladies, do you have some business suits?"

Tarp and Vicky tossed their hair and fluttered hands in front of their faces like old time Hollywood starlets.

"I have a red dress," Tarp said. "I wore it at the Oscars."

They mimed putting on lipstick. Maz smiled and then noticed Butone patting hands in a circle around himself.

"Hey," he looked up. "Where's my gun?"

Let her go.

Jesus ran and ran. His lungs wheezed and legs burned. He turned a corner, unzipped and opened his backpack. The gun was heavy and smooth. All he had to do was point it at Balk and pull the trigger. Balk's head explodes. The Secret Service kills me. My life for the world? Small price.

He zipped the bag and felt an infinite sadness. He hailed a cab and told the driver to pass by his old neighborhood, before going to the Balk rally. Sweating in the backseat, he saw New York pass before his eyes.

Memories flowed like a film reel. He had lost a toy in that gutter. And had his first kiss under that bodega awning.

Let this go. Let this go. Let this go.

It felt like his life was behind thick glass. He told the driver to stop at his corner bodega. Candles flickered by a photo of Muhammad.

"What!" He knelt down. "What the hell happened?"

"Boy got burnt up." An old man swigged a 40-ounce, and pointed his walking cane at the memorial. "Some kids got it into their damn, fool heads that he was a terrorist. Got gassed up on all that Balk shit and..."

His voice faded into the background. A terrible grief roared through Jesus like a subway train. Goddamn Balk. He got back in the taxi. As it pulled away, he saw his building. Up there his parents traded jokes. The TV droned. He wanted to empty the bag on the table, show the gun and tell them about the vampires.

He tore his eyes away and looked forward. If he didn't do this, the war would come. He wiped his mouth. His eyes burned with tears. One image was ablaze in his mind. Balk.

⌄ ⌄ ⌄

"Where is my gun?" Butone shouted. "Where the fuck is my gun?"

Crawling on hands and knees, they peeked under clothes, and near satellite dishes.

"Jesus took it," Maz said.

Butone punched a door. "He took my fucking gun!"

Maz thumbed her temples. Tarp and Vicky traded hopeless glances. The moon was full. Each hour to the election quickly drained away. And now this?

"It's the Knight in Shining Armor routine, right," Sequan said. "He's doing this for you."

Maz shot him a dirty look.

"People. If I can't find my gun. I can't help us," Butone said. "I can't get a detail at the Tower. I'll be knee-deep in paperwork. Do. You. Understand?"

They froze at the idea of Balk as president and pressing the red button.

"There's a rally today." Tarp snapped her fingers.

"He's going there," said Vicky. "If he wants to kill Balk. That's where he'll be. And the gun."

∨ ∨ ∨

Jesus did not like what he saw. Metal fences cordoned the park. Guards waved a magnetic wand over the attendees. Security dogs sniffed people. Police stood every few feet.

"Jesus," someone called.

Raffie waved at him. He wore a Balk shirt, gold teeth. His sister struggled to push a baby stroller next to him.

"Haven't seen you since that party with the pills," Raffie said. "Yo, they took me out the game son, I was gone." He made a fly away gesture.

Jesus faked laughed and gestured to Raffie's sister that he'd push the baby stroller. She wiped the sweat off her forehead and smiled.

"Nigga, look at you being the upstanding gentleman," Raffie said in a low, snide tone. "Who taught you manners?"

Jesus put his backpack on the stroller. The baby whimpered and cried in loud wails that cut the air. Rallygoers online stared. Raffie bounced the infant but it roared.

Jesus trotted to the guards, pointed at the baby, and said it was baking in the sun. They waved all three of them in. He pushed the stroller in.

"Good looking out," Raffie said.

Jesus snatched his backpack and left them behind.

I won't see that baby grow up.

He zig-zagged through the crowd to the podium. The microphone sparkled in the sun. Balk would be there. He squeezed the backpack and felt the gun.

EASE ON DOWN

EASE ON DOWN THE ROAD

Fifteen

"BALK! BALK! BALK!"

Batista was red-faced from shouting. Waves of voices like a stormy ocean, smashed against the podium.

Security guards twitched nervously. What if they breached the metal gates and crashed onto the stage? They'd done it before. Balk encouraged it. Anyone could have a weapon and Balk loved to get close.

"Ladies and gentleman," the speaker said. "I give you the next president of the United States, Ronald Balk!"

"Are we going to make America great again?" Balk strode out, arms wide.

⋏⋎⋏⋎⋏⋎⋏⋎⋏⋎⋏⋎⋏⋎⋏⋎⋏⋎⋏⋎⋏⋎⋏⋎

"YEEEEEESSSSS!"

An ABC news drone circled overhead. Balk gave it the finger. The crowd threw trash at it. They did not like corporate media.

Batista filmed the scene with his cellphone. It wasn't often you were at the center of history. The zoom-lens scanned the immense gathering. He saw Jesus near the podium and nearly dropped the cellphone. Holding it up, he saw Jesus staring at Balk.

"Excuse me." He chopped through the crowd like a machete. "Please. Excuse me."

⌄ ⌄ ⌄

"Goddamn it, pick up." Maz jiggled her cellphone. Jesus was on screen. But no answer.

"He's going to get himself killed," Vicky said.

Butone, Tarp and Sequan wiped sweat from their faces. In the distance, the crowd erupted.

"I can get in," he said. "Keep calling. Talk him down from the ledge. Tell him we can do this together!"

He ran to an entrance and flashed his badge. Security let him. A pained, worried look hung on his face as he jogged to the rally. The line they waited on, inched closer and closer. Guards waved the magnetic wand around torsos. Tarp bit her lip raw.

"If he doesn't stop Jesus, it's all over," she said. "The war will start."

⌄ ⌄ ⌄

Batista saw Jesus edging closer to Balk. Secret Service pointed at him and spoke into their wrists.

Jesus reached into the backpack and pulled out a gun. Shots echoed. Time stopped. Breath stopped. A loud silence froze the crowd. Secret Service jumped in front of Balk. People trampled over each other to escape.

Secret Service men shot the ABC drone. Bullets pinged. Sparks sprayed. The drone wobbled like a wounded dragonfly. It spun and crashed in a smoking wreck.

The crowd stampeded to the exits. Thousands jumped over fences. More shots. Batista saw Jesus and tackled him. They wrestled, blindly. Elbows smashed teeth. Fists punched jaws. Feet kicked feet.

"You don't get it!" Jesus straddled Batista. "You don't know what's going on."

He ran away. Batista tracked the ragged figure of his brother as he vanished. Angrily, he stood and wiped blood off his lips.

"Who are you!" he yelled. "Where's my brother? Where is he?"

ᴠ ᴠ ᴠ

More gunshots. Maz ducked and dodged the terrified stampede. She scanned faces and saw Jesus. They crashed together. His eye was swollen and cheeks scratched bloody.

"I'm sorry," he said. "I'm sorry."

"You love me." She led him to safety.

"You wanted to take the hit. I know. I know." She walked him to a tree. Vicky, Tarp, Butone and Sequan ran over. Butone flung Jesus to the ground. He ripped open the bag, snatched the gun, and kicked Jesus in the ribs.

"Stop it," Maz yelled.

Jesus lay on the dirt, nursing the kick and gasping.

"This fucking guy nearly cost us everything." Butone spat. "Everything!"

Vicky and Sequan pulled him back. Maz stood in front Jesus like a goalie, legs wide and arms out.

"Let it go," Vicky husked. "Let it go."

Butone kicked dirt on Jesus. Tarp, Vicky, and Maz walled off the men who stared hot hate stares.

"We don't have time for this," Maz ordered. "We have to go to Balk Tower. Look up..."

The Super Moon was aglow in the sky. A shudder ran through them. The vampires were strong. They could fly, or slip between shadows. They were close. Everyone had dry lips. The rally must be chock full of them.

"Butone," Maz asked. "Can you get the detail for Balk's Tower?"
"I'll try." He wrung his hands nervously.

"Butone." Maz lowered her voice. "We can't try anymore, feel me, we have hours until the election. I need you to get us inside."

He nodded and stood Jesus up. Face to face, they stared and hate sparked and then in the silent eyeballing, a peace deal was struck. Butone cupped the back of Jesus's neck. He touched their foreheads together.

"I am sorry," he said. "Nigga, I feel you. But you got to promise me we are doing this together. Okay, together."

"Together," Jesus repeated.

"The assassination attempt on Ronald Balk failed." The CNN reporter pointed to police tape. "A drone fitted with a concealed rifled, shot at Balk during his speech." On screen, a blurred photo of the drone appeared. "A radical Left group called The Defiance," he said "...claimed responsibility."

"We're so fucked," Vicky said in a monotone.

"The security is going to be impossible." Maz blinked sarcastically.

Sequan aimed a finger between his teeth and mock-shot himself. He passed the gun-hand to Jesus, who held it to his temple, fake shot himself and slumped on the bench.

"What do, we do?" Tarp asked. Her hands sandwiched between her thighs.

"We go to Liberty City. Meet Butone, get into Balk Tower." Maz rubbed her neck and took a moment to look at everyone. "Find The First One and kill it. After that Balk's spell will be broken. He'll collapse. All of this won't matter anymore, not the assassination, not even the election."

They began a trek from Prospect Park to Balk Tower. Tarp asked to walk because it may her last time seeing New York. They agreed. Vicky had to buy a dress. They passed under the Soldier's and Sailor's Arch that was slashed with angry graffiti. Tiny tornados of trash spun. Knots of angry people, shouted around a trash can filled with bright fire.

Brooklyn, like Manhattan, was battered by the months of rage. Smashed windows looked like broken teeth. Cops gripped military-grade weapons at subway stations. The city had been transformed.

Along the way, they traded childhood stories. Vicky joked about peeing between cars during prom night. Butone guffawed at a story about a plate-throwing fight with his ex-fiancé. Jesus talked about going to his grandparents funeral on that corner. They marveled at what New York City was and what it had become.

Vicky spotted a half-gutted clothing store and they went in. She and Tarp got blazers, and pants to blend in at Balk Tower. Sequan whistled as Vicky spun in the mirror. Maz tried on a black business suit.

"I'm trying for a Matrix look." She play-dodged bullets. They left in new clothes, and a bitter gaiety lifted them. Butone saw an ice-cream store and bought everyone one-scoop cones that melted. So they licked the trickling goo from each other's hands and laughed. On the Brooklyn Bridge, an abandoned couch was left out, so they did the Friends sitcom dance, and sang offkey.

Across the bridge was Manhattan. It loomed like a vast graveyard, and the buildings were tombstones. Quietly, they stared and shared the same thought. Whatever was going to happen to them and to the world, it was going to be settled there, at Balk Tower. None of them thought they'd see another day.

"Ease on down, ease on down the road," Sequan sang. He held out his hand.

"We are not doing The Wiz." Maz frowned.

"Ease on down, ease on down the road." Sequan took Butone and Maz by the arm. They swayed, and the frown cracked into a smile. Maz held Jesus, who grabbed Vicky, who linked with Tarp.

"Don't you carry nothing that could be a load," Butone laid down a nice baritone. "Ease on down the road."

They sang together, a mad, off-kilter chorus, dancing across the Brooklyn Bridge.

v v v

In Columbus Square Circle, Balk appeared on the jumbo screens. The street was packed with people who stared lovingly at him. A cab pulled up. Maz, Butone, Jesus, Vicky, Tarp and Sequan stepped out and carefully tip-toed around the rally.

Vicky got a text that a mass meeting was being held at Liberty City. Should they dissolve the camp? Try to avoid a backlash?

"They country is going bat-shit." Jesus stared wide-eyed at a jumbo screen that showed Balk's poll numbers launching straight up. Newscasters, all but called the election for him.

"If I'm going to get us into Balk Tower," Butone said. "I have to go now."

"Thank you." Maz kissed his forehead. "You know we might not..."

"I know." He hugged her.

"If there's anyone you want to say goodbye to," Maz said.

A knowing look passed between them. It was a hard knowledge of what was to come. He left, took out his phone and dialed his ex-fiancé's number.

Balk heard the chanting. It slammed against his tower like sea tides on rock. The election was tonight. The war would come soon after. It would cleanse this planet of a dead-end species. And the Coven would be freed.

Thirst. Thirst. Thirst.

The voices came. They begged. Cursed. Hoped. Asked. Wondered. Demanded. They lifted Balk. He felt them. Some were near. Some were far away.

Thirst. Thirst. Thirst.

"Who are you?" a soft voice spoke. He turned and saw his wife, hands at her chest, eyes wide. "What are you?"

Balk winked at her. She carefully extended her hand to touch him. He snatched it and dragged her across the room, her legs scissor-kicking. He yanked her across the table. Papers flew up in the air. And he hurled into a shadow.

Blackness blinded her. A brutal, chill wind froze her. She waved hands in front of her face and nothing. At first she ran, then stopped to catch her breath, then ran in any direction. The darkness was infinite. Tired and thirsty, she called for him.

ⱽ ⱽ ⱽ

"You know what to do!" The grizzled man in red, white, and blue overalls waved a torch at the entrance to Central Park.

Raising baseball bats, bicycle chains and knives, Balk voters wanted blood. Batista fingered the brass knuckles on his fist. The cops let them pass. They knew what the deal was. Filthy Leftists tried to kill Balk. Now they would pay.

"BALK! BALK! BALK!"

They punched the air with his name. Batista strode with them. Ahead was a dark-haired woman, tattoos on her neck. Next to him, a short man in a union jacket. Adrenaline lit their brains like kerosene.

Batista dialed Jesus, but stopped the call. Fuck it. Maz. Liberty City. Protesters. They took his brother from him. After tonight, it would all end. Jesus would have to come home and face the family.

"Balk," he shouted the brutal music of the mob. "Balk!"

⌄ ⌄ ⌄

Jesus saw his brother's phone call. A photo of Batista's wide cheeks and goofy smile came up. It was the one he loved best. The call ended. He stared at the blank screen and knew his brother was hurting.

How can I tell you little bro? Would you even listen to me? Could you forgive me for being so shitty?

He dialed his mom. She answered.

"Where are you?"

"Please."

"No. No. Not today. You need to tell me where you are," she demanded. "They are rounding protesters up."

Father barked orders in the background. The phone traded hands.

"Where is your brother, Pendejo?" he screamed. "He's chasing you all over the city!"

"I have to say goodbye." Jesus gripped the phone.

His father cursed and gave the phone back.

"Where are you going?" she asked.

"Do you trust me?" His throat thickened.

She didn't say anything. He waited. So this was it. This was how he let go of life. Forgiveness.

"You were my favorite." she hung up. Hot tears pricked his eyes. Jesus threw the phone into the trees. Maz held him as he wept.

"Want to use my phone?" Vicky held her cell out to Tarp.

"No one to call." She stuffed her hands in the pockets and studied the cracks on the sidewalk.

"You don't want to call anyone?" Vicky insisted. "Say goodbye, say you love them?"

Tarp pushed the phone away. Her family was many years and thousands of miles ago. She ran from screaming, heroin needles, and being sold to strange men. At the mall, activists proselytized about a better world. She followed them to feel love again. Now that was over. She hated Maz for taking that life. If asked, she would've died with everyone else. Not this, on this Mission Impossible, bullshit.

Ahead Vicky cried into her phone. Sobs wrenched her as she said she wasn't coming back and hung up. Maz and Jesus slowed down. Sequan came from his phone call, tear-streaked and hair a mess. They held hands and walked to Liberty City. Tarp trailed behind, arms crossed over her chest.

Bearded men stacked signs on the ground. Couples wrapped themselves in blankets. A woman with cornrows and a megaphone, said a meeting was happening in fifteen minutes.

"Where are the cops?" Sequan scanned the Great Lawn. One or two cops straggled. It felt wrong.

"Hey get in here." Maz waved to the tent. Jesus and Vicky held Super Soaker automatic guns. They bragged about holy water, crosses and the hatchet on the sleeping bag. Maz twisted open the bottle with the last ash swept up from the burning of Charlemagne. Playfully, they stuck their tongues out. The ash boosted their vampire radars. The First One's sheer power gave him away, they could just follow the painful throbbing it caused.

Kneeling, they made the sign of the cross. Maz sprinkled ash on tongues. Licking lips, they hoisted their Super Soaker and pretended to aim at a vampire.

"Balk! Balk! Balk!"

A chant came from the forest, like thunder in the distance. Ears twitched. Quick glances. Maz, Sequan and Vicky stepped outside. A mob emerged from the woods, and waved torches back and forth.

"Butone?" Sequan pressed the phone to his ear. "Butone, what's going on?"

He thumbed the speaker phone. Everyone circled it.

"I just got word," he said. "They are going to let the mob run through the camp and beat anyone they want. More than a few will be plainclothes cops. You gotta get out of there now. Meet me at Balk Tower!"

Protesters picked up signs like clubs. They welded heavy pots and pans. A few flashed knives. Loud commotion rose from the camp's edge. Maz jumped on Jesus's back, to see what was happening. Berserk men plowed tents, swung batons, and kicked whoever fell. It was like watching a rusty-reel lawnmower cutting grass.

"We gotta go," Maz said.

"I'm not." Tarp took a step back. "I never wanted this fight."

The mob charged fast. Faces twisted in ugly hate under torch light. Tents were ripped, and upturned. Jesus, Vicky and Sequan stuffed the Super Soakers, knives and the hatchet into backpacks. Maz stared at Tarp.

"I'm sorry." her lips quivered. "I'm not doing this. I'm tired of everyone making decisions for me!" She ran into the chaos of men and women bumping each other as they fled or went to fight.

Going into the tent, Maz felt the ash heighten her senses. Spit evaporated. Skin itched. The others had large, dilated pupils. The shadows in the tent breathed with a cold wind, as if blowing from across an Arctic tundra. An idea streaked across her mind like a shooting star.

The darkness. Go into the darkness.

"Make a tight circle," she said. "Cover yourselves with anything you can find. Make it as dark as you can. Follow me."

They hugged backpacks, pulled the sleeping bag and blankets over them. Layer after layer, a heavy shell of fabric was made. No light peaked through. The muffled sounds of terrified screams echoed from outside.

Maz felt her nerves burn like white, hot, electric wires. The air was ice in her mouth. She felt them spin and sink as if the earth became quicksand. They plummeted into darkness.

What's going on? What's happening? Why is it so dark? I can't see anything. I can't feel anything.

The mob grabbed protesters and choked them. Gunfire cracked. A man cradled his face as boots came down. Teeth lay on dirt like white pebbles. Angry men slashed Maz's tent and stomped it. The tent fell flat. It was empty.

Batista ran up to it. He saw this tent in the photos Jesus sent. He peeled open the ripped fabric. Nothing. He pressed his hand on the sleeping bag. It felt warm. Someone had been in it just seconds ago. He kicked it aside. Where is my brother?

Where are we?

In the space between. Here is the connected night, the tunnel between space and time that the vampires pass through. Now we can travel here too as long as the ash lasts. When it wears off, we are back in the world.

Hold out your hand. We have to guide each other. Can you feel me?

Yes, I can.

Okay, get your Super Soaker ready and knives. Follow me. We have to go towards the fear, the First One is where the fear resides.

They held onto each other in the blackness. No sound came from their footsteps. Or breathing. Touch guided them. They felt the rise and fall of their limbs, the sweat on their hands. The wind was laced with voices. It blew back and forth in the gloom. The vampires talked in loud, painful laughter.

The endless night, stank of sulfur that stung their eyes. Far away, pinpoints of light opened and closed.

Do you feel the thirst? Do you feel them coming?

Shadows puddled around their feet like a midnight river. They clutched each other's arms or belts. Thirst dried their bodies like beef jerky. Maz urged them forward.

Follow your fear. Go to its source. And kill it.

*In the end,
no one
escaped.*

Sixteen

A BOTTLE SMASHED ON THE WALL.

Foam dribbled down the poster of Vice-President Canton.

"Lock her up!"

Balk voters shot middle fingers at her smiling face and lined up to vote. Beer cans shined in their hands. A woman dressed as a big, foam Super Moon invited squeezes as she swished past them. Everyone knew Balk was going to win.

Butone jogged past the voters to Officer Narros, a burly Dominican man, three years on the force. He began to talk, his esophagus felt like sand. Coughing, he reached for a water bottle and guzzled it.

"You good Butone," Narros asked.

"Yeah, fine." He swiped his bald head. An NYPD car drove up and parked. The Chief of Police got out, and Butone saw his shadow slip under the boots of the Secret Service. He was one of them.

The Chief nodded curtly, then entered Balk Tower. Narros nudged Butone, but he was lost in thought, seeing other shadows slide up the building like liquid silhouettes.

"Trade shifts?" Butone asked Narros.

"Sure." he shrugged.

On the doors of Balk Tower, shadows hi-fived.

∨ ∨ ∨

Where are we?

Jesus, Vicky, Sequan, and Maz made a human chain in the eternal blackness between worlds. Coldness bit their noses. The vampire telepathy, vibrated in a high-pitched humming. Every molecule seemed to shake.

Hold on. Follow me.

Maz pushed like a bull toward the strobe light flashing ahead. Driven by instinct, they stomped one foot in front of the next. They could hear each other in staccato motion. Jesus screamed and fell. Vicky pulled him up by the hair. Sequan and Maz urged them forward. The heavy backpacks slapped their sides. They moved in aching slow-motion toward sickness, dread, and thirst. The strobe punished them. It turned their hair white. It dried skin like prunes. Each blast of light, peeled years off them and exposed them to the endless fathoms of time from which the alien thirst came.

Follow me! Keep Going!

∨ ∨ ∨

The First One ascended to its body like a swimmer up from a deep dive. It blinked. It gasped for air. It flailed in the heaviness of this world. Every atom of air felt like rock. The floor was grimy. Cobwebs hung like drapes and roaches crawled over it. The room was like a small box of blackness, no light, and no sound.

The First One flexed its limbs and felt weak. Its long legs quivered. Arms stirred on the floor. It turned its head and swallowed a bug. Essence. It needed more Essence. The Coven would come and bring more. The First One could feel them coming now.

Out of the shadows, stumbled four humans with white hair. Vicky fished out her cellphone, held it like a lantern above The First One. It hissed and crawled like a crab. They encircled it and pulled out bright Super Soakers.

"We found it," Maz whispered.

The First One looked like a reanimated corpse. Stick thin limbs. Exposed veins and nerves. An open ribcage, where tiny organs flapped like deflated balloons. It was odd. They had lived in terror of it. But it was helpless, disgusting, and bizarre. This was it?

Maz grabbed its ankles and hauled it back. She fired the holy water filled Super Soaker at it. Greasy smoke rose. The others fired their Super Soakers. In the silence, the tiny motors in their water guns pumped.

The First One screamed soundlessly. The pain it felt traveled in a large, concentric circle to the Coven. The agony was raw. Each vampire doubled over, as its mind burst like a lightbulb jolted with too much power.

Maz and Jesus, Vicky and Sequan, shot the damn thing over and over. Here was the one source of the agony in their lives, maybe the source for all of humanity. War. Hunger. Disease. Poverty. Every ill that befell them had been orchestrated by this piece of shit clinging to life as it crawled at their feet. Fuck it. Fuck it to Hell.

"Wait," Maz said.

It writhed on the floor. Limbs whipped back and forth. They kept dousing it.

"Wait," she said again.

They stopped. She took Vicky's cell and passed it up and down its body like a submarine searching the wreck of sunken boat. The First One was in ruins. Shaking in shock, it tried to scoop the parts of itself that dribbled through its ribcage.

"Hatchet," she said.

Jesus gave it to her. Maz drew cutting lines. She pointed the bladed at one shoulder joint, pointed it at thighs and neck.

"Step back." Maz swung the hatchet and cut off the head. She cut loose an arm, cut loose the leg. The blade shined as it fell. Limbs tried to crawl away. Hands groped the floor like sleepy spiders. Feet paddled uselessly. The head moved its mouth.

"I know what we have to do." She picked up the pieces, and dumped them in her backpack. "Let's take it to the reservoir at sunrise. Burn it at sunrise. Scatter its ashes into the water. Eight million New Yorkers will wake up on our side. Then all this is over."

They all grimly smiled. Yes. Hell yes. They savored revenge. Let the masses see the real threat. Let them fight.

A gunshot rang. Blinded by the muzzle flash, they ducked. Maz saw the bullet had gone through the backpack. Coming down the far, far stairs was the Police Chief. He lifted his gun again.

"Come on!" Maz sprinted into a shadow. Jesus, Vicky and Sequan dashed after her. The darkness enveloped them. The panting of their breaths echoed. Bullets whizzed by. They fell, got up, and ran. Bullets kissed the air. A jolt tugged them. "Vicky, let's go." They stopped, and circled back.

"Vicky!" Sequan yelled.

Her moans bounced in the gloom. Where was she? Did she get shot? They pawed the shadow world, slapping around their feet. But the vampire buzzing returned. It was like being inside a beehive.

Maz yanked them forward. Sequan dug heels in but they dragged him. Maz sensed an opening and dove into a purple-tinged shade. They fell in and tumbled out onto the floor of a stairwell in Balk Tower.

"Vicky," Sequan cried. "Vicky!"

⌄ ⌄ ⌄

Blood bubbled from her stomach. It was warm and sticky on her hands. Vicky pressed down on the wounds. Her pulse throbbed a little less with every heartbeat. She panicked. The inky void was total. The silence was total. Nothing existed here.

Vicky wiped her face and accidentally slicked it with blood. She laughed at her clumsiness, but the laughter hurt. Is this how it ends?

Her heartbeat ebbed away. She got sleepy and warm. Oh my God. Death is peaceful? Who knew?

⌄ ⌄ ⌄

"We gotta get the fuck out of here." Maz shook Sequan. He blinked rapidly, as if his brain was resetting. Yes. Run. Vampires.

"No one." Jesus peeked up the stairs. "Can we shadow travel again?"

Maz unzipped the bag, held up the First One's severed head. It snapped at her like a mean turtle. She shook it fiercely.

"How do we get out?" she demanded.

It smiled weakly. Maz smacked it against the wall. She brought the head back.

"How the fuck do we get out?" she snarled.

The First One whispered. Jesus leaned in and it chomped his ear. Maz tore it free. Jesus cupped his chewed lobe. The First One giggled.

Sequan punched it like a boxing bag. Maz stopped his useless rage and stuffed the head into the backpack. Behind her a shadow crawled. Jesus told her to duck. Sequan hit it with the hatched. A vampire materialized, a deep red cut in its skull. It fell.

"Up." Maz gestured. "To the roof. I have a plan."

They leapt three stairs at a time. One long, twisted, panicked flight punctuated by looks over the shoulder. On the other side of the exit door windows, security guards stood. How do we get out? how do we not get killed? They needed another dark stairwell, a shadow to go in like a door, and escape Balk Tower.

"No place is dark enough," Jesus said.

A dark shadow clawed at them. He aimed the Super Soaker and shot. A vampire dropped from thin air, holding a smoky face. More shadows crawled on walls. Sequan, Jesus and Maz formed a triangle and sprayed them with the Super Soakers. Vampires dropped and clutched scalded skin. They melted into gooey sticky puddles.

"Keep running," Maz said.

They ran up corkscrew stairs and fired holy water. The Super Soakers were lighter, and the streams were weak.

Maz took the hatchet from Sequan and smashed the fluorescent light. Blackness descended. They seized hands and leapt into a shadow. It felt like jumping into a canyon. They fell, and fell, and fell.

Balk hurled a chair. He couldn't see. He couldn't hear. The telepathic connection vanished like a thread cut by a knife.

He sat by the window, a large, bright Super Moon painted Manhattan in frosty, pale light. He sighed. Election night was the start of immortality. He would be President and start the war. But where was The First One?

The Chief emerged from a shadow, with wide panicked eyes. He clutched slick blood and let loose a monstrous moan.

"They stole our Master," he said.

"Who stole?" Balk slapped the Chief. "Who?"

Handprints thumped on glass. The Coven arrived. Naked men and women materialized out of the shadows. Balk stood, ready to go with them between worlds to The First One. Shouts came from a dark corner. Three youth tumbled out. Each one had white hair, wrinkled skin, and orange Super Soakers.

Quickly, they scrambled to their feet. Sequan collapsed on the floor. He held a broken foot that jutted to the side at an ugly angle.

"You," Maz scowled.

"Who." Balk spat on the floor. "Are you?"

In one fluid motion, she drew from the backpack The First One's dripping head. Every one held still. One by one, the vampires buckled to their knees. Shame and sorrow reverberated in the room, as they like children looked on, seeing a destroyed parent.

Jesus nudged Maz to the plate-glass doors. Upstairs was the roof. They carefully backed away. Each step they took was matched by the vampires, who moved closer. The oddly-morbid dance stretched painfully over raw nerves, until Maz saw a shadow creep near Sequan and drag him to the Coven. They devoured him.

"NOOOOOOOO!" Maz fired holy water.

Jesus broke open the glass doors and shoved her through. Maz saw Sequan's head fall like a bucket of sand.

On the roof, cool wind whipped them. New York glittered below. The moon was huge and bright. Shadows circled them.

Maz and Jesus doggedly held ground. Balk stepped on the broken glass. Vampires followed him. Rage corkscrewed their faces. The Chief aimed his gun at them.

"Give us the backpack!" veins throbbed on Balk's neck. "We won't kill you."

The vampires panted.

"They needed a willing host," Maz shouted. "I was never willing. Why did you do it Balk? Why were you going to kill us to join them?"

"Look at this small, petty world." He swept one arm in a theatrical wave. "We have a chance to evolve. Shed this dirty monkey flesh. We can live forever!"

"You're a fool," she said. "They are cannibals. They eat worlds. They eat species. And they'll eat you too."

Balk charged like a bull. Speeding across the half-finished rooftop, he jumped at Maz. Jesus punched him. The men wrestled. Balk took a hammer left by the crew and struck Jesus. Jets of blood spritzed from the cracked skull. He woozily tried to stand. Balk roughly walked him to the roof's edge and threw him over.

"Jesus!" Maz held out her hands, as if to reel him back. She silently mouthed his name. And blinked in shock.

On the dark roof, hungry eyes saw her weakness. The rubbed hands like flies at the edge of a plate. It was over. She was goddamn tired. They had won. The vampires had dark veins that were throbbed under translucent skin. Their eyes grew large like insect eyes and needle teeth jutted from gums.

Maz looked at her own hands, they glittered with moonlight. It was better that Jesus did not see what she was going to do. A wave of grief broke, and she could almost feel his head on her lap. *Okay, if it's over, then let's fucking end it.*

Maz unzipped the backpack, lifted The First One's head, and kissed it. She tongued every bit of blood, and flesh she could from it. The mob of vampires, Balk and the Chief froze in place. She wiped her mouth. Her brain jerked as if zapped by lightning.

Moonlight passed into her like light penetrating the water's surface.

She felt weightless. Wind lifted her onto her tiptoes. And into the air.

Two vampires clawed at her sneakers. Acidic hate bubbled in her heart. Maz stretched out her hand and squeezed it into a fist. The two vampires who chased her grabbed their chests and spun down to the roof. Balk threw the hammer and she gently avoided it.

"We will find you." Balk pointed at her. "And kill you."

The wind lifted Maz into a low cloud.

"I'll see you in hell." She laughed and became a blurry smudge in the sky. The vampires flew after her.

Butone drove the NYPD cruiser as drunks smeared their faces on the window. A joyful mob rocked a news van, and reporters tumbled out.

"Balk! Balk! Balk!"

Please help.

It was Maz. She called him telepathically. He tried to focus above the racket of the election parties. A woman rubbed tits on the windshield. Fucking idiots.

Please help.

Butone steered through the crowds. Where is she? Damn it. He followed her voice, but it was fading. Hopeless despair sank in his belly as he drove. He parked near an alley, got out and searched it with a flashlight. A boot stuck out between garbage bags. Under a cardboard box was Maz. She was bruised, dirty but clutching the backpack. He lifted her with infinite gentleness and laid her in the backseat of the cruiser.

"Drive upstate," she husked.

He drove out of New York City. Along the way, he saw Balk's face on posters, and voters singing the National Anthem. The highway of night, was a metronome of white lines on dark asphalt. The windows were down, and cool air kept him awake. In the back, Maz lay half asleep.

"Neversink reservoir," she mumbled.

Butone nodded. She turned on the radio.

"President Elect Ronald Balk will be holding a rally in..." the CNN anchor said. She turned it off.

"The others," Butone asked.

Maz shook her head. Tears salted his eyes. Butone blinked hard and focused on the road.

⌄ ⌄ ⌄

He parked on the road side. They climbed over the reservoir fence and down rocks to the tides slapping rocks. The low moon sparkled like a diamond dress floating on the lake. Maz and Butone sat for a moment to take in the beauty.

"I haven't felt calmness in a long time," Maz said. "Thought I'd never experience it."

"Me too." He put his arm around her. She lay on his shoulder. They sighed. He touched her white hair. Maz fingered the strands.

"I aged." she laughed.

"I guess I don't need to card you to get into clubs," he teased. They laughed. The thin glow of sunrise rose from the horizon. Birds woke up and filled the air with music. Maz realized the lovely sound was all she heard. No voices. No dry mouth. Nothing.

"Do you feel quiet inside," she asked.

"I do," he said.

The dawn brightened the sky. Butone patted her back. It was time. Maz slipped off her clothes and waded into the water. She held the backpack up. The wide reservoir was a mirror of the sky. It was like walking on clouds.

The First One squirmed inside and Mas took out its arms. Sunlight broke. They sizzled to dust. Next were its legs. They burst. She tossed the empty backpack to Butone. The First One's head was in her hands. She raised it to the sun. Fire erupted from its ears, mouth and eyes. The flames singed her hands.

Maz saw her reflection on the water, holding a ball of fire. She drew her hands down. Wind scattered the ash across the reservoir. It was over.

She floated away. The sounds of the lake's depths echoed in her ears. The sky was radiant with new color. So was she.

EPILOGUE

Days later, Batista ran to the Balk victory rally. Of course, he was late. And oddly thirsty. On the subway, he met friends and they shared a water bottle.

Worry ate at Batista like termites. He taped a smile over the fear that his brother was gone. Besides Balk had won! Now the work of repairing America could start. The rally was at Central Park, a way to stomp on the memory of Liberty City.

But he was dizzy. He used the handrail to climb the subway station steps. He saw other people rub their temples. A man stopped on the sidewalk, and shouted for everyone to get out of his head. Everyone walked around him.

Batista and his friends hurried into Central Park. The woods rang with joy at the election victory. Between high fives and smiles, he saw people pop aspirin. Or palm foreheads. The vibe was off. Attendees sat on the dirt, shaking their heads.

Dryness caked his mouth. God it hurt. Like his throat was sandpaper. He tried to ignore it and took out his cell. Jesus face was the screen saver. His finger hovered over the call button. A cheer from the crowd distracted him.

"Balk! Balk! Balk!"

The man of the hour walked on stage, but Balk nearly tripped on his own feet. The crowd's energy was erratic. A painful scream tore the air. Three men held another man, who stabbed his ears with a pen. Near him, a woman vomited.

Batista swigged the water bottle, and a high-pitched shrill drilled into his brain. He spun in blind circles. People around him collapsed.

Balk tried to speak, but the crowd reeled at the sound of his voice. Cops onstage yanked off helmets and slapped their heads. A great agony rose from the masses as he talked. Each syllable scraped them like a knife.

Batista got a text from his mother that showed a banker set on fire. He tried to see it, but a headache rattled him. The image wobbled. More followed. Wealthy people were being killed across the city.

When Batista looked up, he saw Balk trying to control the crowd. The moment froze like a film that stopped midway and began to burn. The face of the man they worshipped was gone, in its place was an alien thing with large, insect-like eyes, and a mouth filled with needle teeth. It twitched helplessly.

Pain pounded his brain to jelly. The thing on stage ate their pain. It devoured their pain. It thirsted for their pain. A wild, animal hate lifted every face. They could feel this parasite had lived inside their souls.

Aides reached for Balk with murder in their eyes. The crowd climbed the podium. Cops rushed in. They tore him limb from limb. Out of the turmoil, Balk's head rolled like a football down the stage steps. And in the people's faces was a holiness.

In the dirt, Batista's phone showed scenes of mobs rampaging through police stations, banks and corporations. They would point at men or women who tried to run but would get tackled down. The vampires were visible. And the people, with a gleeful, grunting passion, stomped them to death.

CREDITS

Various excerpts have been incorporated into the artwork of each chapter.
They are recognized and credited appropriately below.

CHAPTER ONE

Excerpt from "*Chupacabra*" by **Cage** on <u>Darker Than Black</u>.
Massacre Records, 2003; Catalog ID: MAS CL0343

CHAPTER TWO

Excerpt from "*Comfortably Numb*" by **Pink Floyd** on <u>The Wall</u>.
Harvest Records, 1979; Catalog ID: SHDW 411

CHAPTER THREE

Excerpt from "*Communion*" by **Fiona Sampson** as appears in <u>Poetry Magazine</u>.
Poetry Foundation (pub.), January 2009 issue; Chicago.

CHAPTER FOUR

Excerpt from "*To London*" by **Vahni Capildeo** from <u>Measures of Expatriation</u>.
Carcanet Press, 2016.

CHAPTER FIVE

Excerpt from <u>Das Kapital. Kritik der politischen Ökonomie</u> by **Karl Marx**.
Verlag von Otto Meisner (pub.), 1867.

CHAPTER SIX

Excerpt from "*The Wall*" by **Alfred Corn** on <u>Unions</u>.
Barrow Street Press, 2014.

CHAPTER SEVEN

Excerpt from "*Revelations*" from <u>King James Bible</u>.
Various publication sources.

CHAPTER EIGHT

Excerpt from "*Shadows*" by **Jayanta Mahapatra** as appears in <u>Poetry Magazine</u>.
Poetry Foundation (pub.), April 1977 issue; Chicago.

CHAPTER NINE

Excerpt from "*Who Wants To Live Forever*" by **Queen** on <u>A Kind of Magic</u>.
EMI, 1986; Catalog ID: EU 3509 - 24 0531 1

CHAPTER TEN

Excerpt from "*Diving into the Wreck*" by **Adrienne Rich an Francis Driscoll**
on <u>Diving into the Wreck: Poems 1971–1972</u>. W.W. Norton & Company, 1973.

CHAPTER ELEVEN

Excerpt from <u>The Crowd: A Study of the Popular Mind</u> by **Gustave Le Bon**.
T. Fisher Unwin (pub.), 1896; London

CHAPTER TWELVE

Phrase commonly attributed to **Sergey Nechayev**, 19th century Russian revolutionary.

CHAPTER THIRTEEN

Excerpt from <u>Human, All Too Human</u> by **Friedrich Nietzsche**.
Ernst Schmeitzner (pub.), 1878.

CHAPTER FOURTEEN

Excerpt from <u>Hard-Boiled Wonderland and the End of the World</u> by **Haruki Murakami**.
Kodansha International, 1985; Japan.

CHAPTER FIFTEEN

Excerpt from "*Ease on Down the Road*" by **Charlie Smalls** on
<u>The Wiz: Original Motion Picture Soundtrack</u>. MCA, 1978.